the Wish House

Celia Rees

YOUNG PICADOR

FIC

First published 2005 by Young Picador

This edition published 2006 by Young Picador
an imprint of Pan Macmillan Ltd
20 New Wharf Road, London N1 9RR
Basingstoke and Oxford
www.panmacmillan.com

Associated companies throughout the world

ISBN-13: 978-0-330-43643-4
ISBN-10: 0-330-43643-0

1 3 5 7 9 8 6 4 2

A CIP catalogue record for this book is available from
the British Library.

Typeset by Intype Libra Ltd
Printed and bound in Great Britain by Mackays of Chatham plc, Kent

The Wish House

They walked in the soft sand, through tufts of grey-green spiky marram grass with only the cold moon to guide them. They found a deep place, sliding down the steep banks, landing in a heap at the bottom. The sand was cool and silky to the touch. Clio spread the rug and beckoned him down beside her. He leaned over her, stroking strands of fine hair away from her face. She was pale in the moonlight, her lips slightly parted. He leaned closer, kissing her lightly, then more deeply and, at that moment, he did not care a whole lot what she'd done . . .

For Julia

I would like to thank:
Terry, as always, for all his help and support.
Also Osi and Hilary Rhys Osmond, for help
with details about Welsh and Art.

You are invited to the

PRIVATE VIEW

CLIO DALTON:
Art bleeds Art
(mixed media)

ANDREW FISHER:
Stone (d)
(ceramics)

ANGELA GIBBONS:
mother 2 another
(textiles)

Thursday, 10th June 1982

6 p.m. to 8 p.m.

To be opened by
CHARLES HAMMOND

at
GALLERY X

5 D'Arblay St

Soho

London W1

Tubes: Oxford Circus, Tottenham Court Road, Piccadilly Circus

Admission only with invitation

Admits two

THE SUMMER OF THE WISH HOUSE

Richard still thought about it like that, in standout large letters, capitalized in his mind. Title to a very special time. The end of his childhood. Richard had been fifteen that year, a good enough age to begin being an adult, but maybe the transition from one stage of life to another wasn't marked by passing years, but by some event. Like the first time you did something: first drink, first smoke, first toke, first real kiss, first true love, first sex.

First death.

Whatever. There had been all that, and more. Good enough reasons to stop being a child. That's if childhood ends at all. Some people don't think that it does. They think that the child stays curled up inside us forever. Richard left Tottenham Court Road tube station and began making his way into Soho. He took the creased invite from his pocket to check the map on the back. He thought that he knew Soho pretty well, but it was easy to get confused in the maze of little streets. He turned the card in his hands and looked at the street signs, reorienting himself before he set off again, more confident now. He stuffed the invitation into his pocket again and went back to examining his thoughts, turning them round in his mind, handling them delicately, amazed that they were even coming to him at all. A makeshift mosaic of shame and guilt had built up inside. Shutting them down had become automatic.

He approached the gallery slowly, head down, shoulders hunched, hands bunched in his pockets. He ducked into the entrance to a little mews across the street. He didn't want to go into the goldfish bowl world he could see through the big glass window just yet, but he knew he would have to. He was here to make sure. The child inside him did not sleep secure.

He watched the people moving about, weaving like fish through and around each other and the various little plinths and columns, pausing momentarily in front of some exhibit before moving on to the next. He willed himself not to look for her, but picked her out easily in the restless melee of punks, goths and swaggering New Romantics. Many of the people around her had their hair in spikes, or flossed out and died purple, pink or blue. She'd had her hair cut to chin length since the last time he saw her, but it still fell straight and swung as she turned her head, as black and shiny as liquorice straps. She looked that much older, but then he supposed he did, too. She was thin, the high laced work boots looked heavy on her slender legs, but she was full-breasted, like her mother. Her body looked frail and womanly at the same time inside the retro dress with the deliberate tears around the hem and at the shoulder. Some of the sweetness had gone from her face. The cheekbones were more prominent, her full lips painted a deep purple colour, her violet eyes made huge by mascara and thick black liner.

He approached the gallery apprehensively, crossing the narrow street with something like fear. Why *had* she invited him? What was she after? Coming to the kerb, his footsteps faltered. Surely, he was mad to come here. Crazy. Like tearing at a wound almost healed. Why open himself to further injury?

He went over to the window. It had been six years since he'd seen her. That last encounter came back as vividly as if it had only just happened. The cold rain falling down; the strong, scorched smell of earth after long drought. The things that he'd done. The way he'd got it all so wrong. The hideous embarrassment. He nearly turned back, convinced that, even after all this time, he still could not face her. And there were things she didn't know. Things he would have to tell her.

He'd thought that he could cope, but all his thinking, all his planning had not prepared him for her actually being this close. It was like a sudden blow aimed at the centre of him. He felt it go through him, tingling down his legs and up into his chest, an almost physical pain which left him light-headed. There was more to it than just his guilt. He could sense her power, her magic, even through the thick plate glass. He was caught by it again, and a sudden fear sent him cold and made him shiver, despite the oppressive evening heat. Maybe he never would recover, maybe she was in his blood forever, a fever that would recur and recur all through his life, like malaria. Maybe that's what Jay had meant. He could almost hear the dead artist's voice, a growling whisper deep in his ear. *Go, boy. Get away while you still can. You don't have to do this.*

He took a step back, making as if to walk away, as though he'd never intended to go in anyway. But he stayed, watching her through the window.

He thought he heard Jay's jeering laugh: *Don't say I didn't warn you!*

She blended with the people circling around her, an art student just out of college, but she was not really like the rest of them. There was a notoriety about her. Her story was the kind people liked to repeat to each other. Her father, J. A. Dalton, the well-known artist, not exactly a national treasure but not far off it. His bizarre death. So sudden. All those paintings. All that money. And her so young.

Richard remembered his shock on reading the details of the inquest into the artist's death. The names, the facts, the circumstances had leaped out at him from the newspaper pages. A worst dread realized. A nightmare come true. Actually seeing it all set out made it real in a way it hadn't been before. It made him feel quite sick. He'd gripped the paper, scanning the columns, his fingers printing the pages with dampness. Even now, it made his stomach churn to recall it.

He'd followed the story in private, buying his own paper, locking himself in the toilet to read it. He'd been astounded by the final verdict: 'Death by misadventure', 'Weird people do weird things.' That is what the coroner seemed to suggest. They thought it was an accident, but Richard still felt guilty, even now, as though it had all been his fault somehow. What if her brother Joe was here? Or her mother, Lucia?

What he should really do was walk on down the street without looking back. He stared up at the gallery front. It had been a shop until quite recently. The original sign: Grisham & Sons, Bespoke Tailoring and Gentlemen's Attire showed faint below the silver on white Gallery *X* design. Across the road, lurid neon winked on and off above an 'Adult Interest' bookshop. The area was kind of scruffy, but full of character. Cool and alternative. Up and coming, but still dodgy enough to retain street cred. Trust her to pick a place like that.

It was a private view, but he wouldn't have to blag his way past the guy on the door. He held up the invitation, sent on from home. He wondered how she had known his address. He didn't remember ever telling her. But if she wanted it, she'd find it. She was that kind of girl. She must have found out specially. That thought made his nerves tingle even more.

He blended in without any problem. Not all her art student friends were punks and he was just another guy dressed in black, his long hair tied back. She was standing deep in conversation with a group of people. As he came in, she looked up and for a second their eyes met. She nodded and gave a wide smile that made his heart jump. She mouthed something he couldn't hear, her teeth very white against the purple lipstick, her big eyes bright and slightly mocking. Richard remembered that look very well. She was detaching herself from the group she had been with, moving towards him through the crowded room, causing him to search frantically through his mind for one of the phrases that he had prepared and ready. He was all set to stammer out the words when someone took her arm, steering her away from him. She turned her head, pouting her lips, as if blowing a kiss, her mouth shaping what he thought might be 'Later' and '*Ciao*, Ricardo.'

No one had called him that since that summer. Richard felt suddenly weak. He looked round for a wall, somewhere to lean, and found some stairs which seemed to lead up to nowhere. He had to get a hold of himself. He sat down and opened his programme with shaking fingers:

This exhibition is not an exhibition in the accepted sense. The exhibition *is* the work. An installation that has to be viewed as a whole concept within its space. Just as . . .

Then came a list of artists and installations. Richard had never heard of any of them. He read on, retreating to his fallback position, the one he'd worked out for if she completely ignored him. He had a way of distancing himself. He wanted to be a journalist after he had finished his degree. He might write this up for the student paper. This is just a story, he told himself. Just a story. See what happens. See where it takes me.

A frown creased his forehead as he turned the page. He was having difficulty working out what the paragraphs of clotted prose meant. Loud music supplied by a live band that had set up down the far end of the gallery did not help all that much.

What are they *doing here making a bloody racket? This is an art gallery, for God's sake, not a discotheque.* Richard could hear Jay's voice again. He looked down at the notes in his hand. Maybe he really was going mad. *Don't bother reading that claptrap. You're not in a library. Didn't you listen to anything I told you? Look at the art, lad. Look at the art!*

Richard did just that.

Across the room, people were jostling each other, trying to get close to one particular exhibit. Richard stood up, curious to know what was causing the interest. He mounted the steps. The stairs gave him height enough to see over all their heads. There was a notice in big red letters:

WARNING: EXPLICIT CONTENT

Of all the exhibits in the room, this was causing the most stir. It looked as though Clio would soon be notorious in her own right. The illustrations were clear and graphic, in the instantly recognizable style of J. A. Dalton. People gasped, oohed and aahed, telling each other about 'Innocence. Purity. Breathtaking beauty of line,' while trying to edge close enough to get an even better look and to read the accompanying text. Richard did not join the throng. He stayed where he was. He'd seen the images before. The content did not shock him; he'd viewed his share of pornography, it was just that he did not normally have a starring role. He was not scared that anyone would recognize him. That seemed unlikely with his clothes on. He thought he'd destroyed every image in that particular series. The shock came from seeing them at all.

He dragged his gaze away and forced himself to look down at the programme.

Exhibits 9a & 9b
Clio Dalton has added her own commentary to her father's wonderfully subversive Beardsleyesque pen-and-ink drawings. She writes in the manner of a medieval chronicle, but the writing takes the form of a relentlessly pornographic monologue. The text is beautifully executed but overwritten, the words running horizontally and vertically at the same time, giving the effect of urgency, laying one experience on top of another, with the seemingly deliberate intention of obscuring each one from the viewer, revealing and concealing to produce a density of meaning in a way that is already emerging as signature for this exciting young artist.

What did *that* mean?

Search me, Jay's whisper came back. *But you can't get rid of art as easy as that, lad.*

He might have known.

This was a private view so there was wine. Richard went over to a rickety table holding a few two-litre screw-top bottles. He needed to steady himself and might as well take advantage of the free booze. They'd run out of red already, so Richard took a glass of white. It was warm, looked like piss and tasted similar, but he downed that one, then another.

A sign on the wall above his head said:

> The elements that make up the whole do not have to be
> viewed in any order. Randomness is crucial in this con-
> text, replicating the meaningful/meaningless interface
> that continually confronts the artist . . .

Richard looked around. The others here might know what
that meant, but he didn't understand a word. I've had
enough of this, he thought as he wiped his hand across the
back of his mouth. I'm off to the pub.

The gallery was small. To allow more hanging space, it
had been set out in a series of panels put at angles to each
other. Richard knocked off another glass of wine and made
for where he figured the door to be, but the panel labyrinth
and the crowds of people had a disorienting effect. He
turned a corner and walked straight into a life-sized portrait of himself.

Caught you! Jay's deep voice crooned in his ear. *You can't
leave now!*

Richard Entering the Garden

(1976) Oil on canvas (unfinished)

182 x 152 cm

Tate Collection

Jethro Arnold Dalton R.A. (1916–1976)

Dalton was working on this painting at the time of his sudden death. The figure of the boy dominates the foreground. He is stepping into the garden, frozen in motion and a moment in time, reaching backwards with one hand and at the same time forwards, his body casting a deep shadow over the figure stretched out on the lawn. The boy's classical quality, the smooth pale skin and rounded limbs, suggests a young Apollo and is perhaps an ironic reference to the work of John Dalton. However, the mundane clothing (khaki shorts, aertex shirt, striped pullover, grey socks, leather sandals) adds the realism that makes this unmistakably the work of J. A. Dalton rather than his father. As in many of his paintings, Dalton prefers mystery and resists straightforward narrative, but the beautiful solidity of the limbs and the pallid flesh tones suggest a universality of theme: the moment of transition from boyhood to manhood. The house (the Wish House, Dalton's home in South Wales) is another solid presence. Painstakingly depicted, strong sunlight reflects from the glass and bleaches the grey stone to blank, blinding whiteness against the dark greens of the trees and the deep blues of the sky.

(From catalogue notes: Dalton retrospective, 1980)

Richard had never seen a naked woman before. Not in real life. He'd only seen pictures on the creased pages of magazines that boys brought into school, or between the covers of the copies of *Playboy* and *Penthouse* that his father kept locked up in the bottom drawer of his desk. This woman didn't look like them. She was golden all over. No bikini marks marred the smooth expanse of her skin. She lay with one arm flung out on the crisping grass, the other shading her eyes from the sun. Her hair was spread out around her head in a vibrant red corolla. A shade that his mother would no doubt condemn as '*Never* natural!'

He froze in mid-step, intensely aware of his own paleness encased in hairy wool and khaki. He had not expected anyone to be here when he mounted the worn steps up to the garden. The big grey stone house had been deserted when he had come here with Dylan last summer. It had been empty for years and had become one of their special places, where they went to play and explore. It was called the Wish House, Dylan had told him, because the trees around it seemed to be in constant motion. Even on a day as still as this, they seemed to whisper, 'I wish . . ., I wish . . .' It gave the house an extra creepiness that added spice to their visits. The sound was there now, mixed in with thin-sounding, slightly discordant music made by stringed instruments and a drum. That was what had made Richard mount the steps, thinking he'd discovered something genuinely mysterious – until he saw this woman.

He tried to look away, but he couldn't shift his focus. He

13

held his hand up, as if to ward off the vision, or to block off his own line of sight. He reached behind, as though to steady himself on the warm lichen-embossed wall. He was beginning to sweat. He felt the dampness creeping through his hair, the beads break out on his forehead and upper lip. Should he go on? Should he go back? He did not know what to do.

The decision was made for him.

The woman rose up on one elbow, squinting at him, shading her eyes against the strong sun shining from behind him, the glare of light shimmering up from the sea.

'Well, hello there. And who are you?'

She made no attempt to cover herself, just reached for her sunglasses and leaned back.

'My name, my name is . . .'

He'd temporarily forgotten and, anyway, the words wouldn't come out. His voice had been reduced to a reedy croak. He stared, dry-mouthed, at the gilded skin, the spun-gold fuzz, then up to the black oval eyes staring back at him. Her smile widened. His face flushed a dull, beet red.

'Rick, Ricky, Richard.' He groped for a version of his name that didn't sound childish. Stupid.

'Well, Rickrickyrichard –' she gave a deep throaty laugh and rose in one fluid movement, twitching a filmy, silky length of blue and green material up from the drying grass – 'I will call you Ricardo.'

She rolled the 'R' and put the emphasis on the middle syllable. Her voice was husky, low and musical. It made his name sound suddenly exciting and exotic. She wrapped the cloth around herself, knotting it into a kind of sari, and came forward to meet him. Her step was light. She seemed to float over the grass.

'My name is Lucia. *Ciao, bambino.*' She pronounced her

name in the Italian way, with a 'ch' in the middle. 'Do you like the music? It's Moroccan. My son, Joe, has set up a system. We shall have music wherever we go.'

She trilled the last words as she came towards him. There were speakers in the windows. Richard could see them now. He fought down a desire to wipe his own sweating palm on his shorts as he took her proffered hand. Her fingers were slim, and heavy with silver rings, the nails painted the same bright red as her lipstick. Her hand was dry, while his was as wet as a fish.

'Hot, isn't it?' She smiled at him. Her teeth were small and white with a gap in the middle. She wore a jewel in the side of her nose. 'I expect you could do with a drink. I know *I* could. Why don't you come in? You must be melting in that tank top.'

She still held his hand, but loosely now, leading him towards the dark opening of the door. A sound from above made Richard look up. He squinted against the strong light bouncing off the grey weathered stone and winking from the windowpanes on this south-facing side of the house. The roof lowered down over a series of small jutting gables, the mottled stone tiles arching like eyebrows. The window of the central gable was flung open and a girl was leaning on the sill, looking down at him. Her arms were bare and her black hair swung forward, silver in the sun; her dark eyes sparked with mischief. She had seen the whole thing and she was laughing. At him.

Jay saw him before Clio. She had been posing with her back to the outside world and was suddenly aware that he was not looking *at* her, but over her shoulder. She turned to see what could have attracted him. Voices floated in: a boy announcing himself: 'Rick, Ricky, Richard . . .', Lucia's

15

throaty chuckle in reply. Clio smiled. Overwhelmed, no doubt, by the sight of a naked Lucia, he couldn't even get his own name right. She left her place, going to the open window, staying to watch the comic tableau being acted out below her.

Jay stared at her for a moment, his head cocked on one side as he examined the way she was standing. His fingers twitched as he noted the exact angle of her head, the sweep of her neck, the crook of her elbow resting on the sill. Only then did he follow her over to look out of the window. He stood behind her, brooding and still. He clearly did not seem to find the scene in the garden as amusing as she did. She glanced up to see that his jaw was set rigid, his skin quite pale.

'I want him,' he said, gripping her arm, badging her bare skin with paint.

'Him?' Clio laughed even more as the boy passed under the window, led through the door by Lucia. He looked like a Hereford bull calf being taken in for slaughter. 'What could you possibly want with him?'

Jay continued to stare, although the boy had disappeared into the house by now.

'I just do, that's all.' His hold on her tightened.

The pinch caused tears to start in her eyes, but she endured the pain. There was no point in protesting, he probably wouldn't even hear if she did. He was in another place, gazing abstractedly at the space where the boy had been.

Clio knew the signs. Lucia would be overjoyed. In her capacity as arch-muse and helper, she would see this as a rekindling of the sacred fire of his creativity. He rarely painted Lucia now. His interest had passed to Clio years ago, but recently his enthusiasm even for her seemed to have cooled, dying down to so much ash. He had been fired up when she first got back from school. They'd gone up to the studio every day, but so far nothing had come of it. He would often dismiss her, after only a couple of minutes, and stay on alone, brooding and bitter. Or else he would mess around mixing colours, like today, but with no sign of getting started. Or he would set about making drawings, only to tear them up before they were completed, working himself into a rage. He had painted nothing for months. His studio occupied the whole top storey of the house and Clio could hear him pacing at night, up and down, up and down, well into the morning hours.

Clio pulled away from his grip and grabbed her wrap. That kid will bring trouble, she thought with sudden intuition, or perhaps it was just the pain, spilling into resentment towards the boy, and towards Lucia for her tendency to pick up strays.

Jay stayed at the window, arms folded, while Clio melted away from him. He'd dismissed her already and was thinking about the boy. The resemblance was uncanny, even the name . . .

Who was he? Why had he come here? Why now? It had to mean something. It had to be important. Jay did not believe in magic, unlike Lucia with her crystals and tarot, but he did believe in fate, in destiny. Perhaps the past had finally caught up with him. Which meant there could be no escaping. Whatever would be, would be. All he knew for sure was that he had to paint this boy. He had felt the old excitement igniting deep within him. It burst in his brain, heady as champagne, and tingled down through his wrists, making the joints of his fingers ache, the tips itch. He clasped his hands tightly together to control the slight tremor that had started. It was the excitement, he told himself. It had to be.

Even while he was feeling this, part of him was already experiencing a kind of sorrow, preparing for the disappointment that he knew would follow. Nothing was ever how you thought it was going to be. That is what drove one on, day after day, painting after painting. Trying to create perfection; knowing that nothing could ever match that first creative flash.

Inside the Cave of Enchantment

(1969) Collage

90 x 53.12 cm

Walton Collection

Jethro Arnold Dalton R.A. (1916–1976)

Dalton was a great admirer of the Pre-Raphaelites and their followers – whose numbers include his father, John Dalton (1876–1948) – and he shared many of their interests, both in matters of technique and subject. In this painting, he combines aspects of Anthony Fredrick Augustus Sandys' (1829–1904) *Morgan le Fay* and *Medea*. His muse, his wife Lucia, poses in the dramatic fashion of Morgan, cloaked and gowned in skins and garments marked with magical runic symbols, mixing potions made of the poisonous substances clearly placed around her. She works in a dark timeless interior filled with a witch's paraphernalia. Images cut and torn from women's magazines: pots and pans, an ironing board, a laundry basket, an Aga cooker, mark an unusual (for Dalton) departure into mixed media and are an ironic comment on his wife's arcane interests, her persona as a self-styled witch and her comparative indifference to mundane housework.

(From catalogue notes: Dalton retrospective, 1980)

It was dark as a cave inside the house. Richard's eyes took a while to adjust. What he eventually saw amazed him. The place had been shut up for as long as he remembered, as long as they'd been coming here on holiday. When he'd been in with Dylan last year they had wandered through the beginnings of a ruin. The rain had been getting in where slates had fallen from the roof and the wood panelling had begun to spring from the walls, bending outwards in delicate fanning falls. The stone flags had been mired with bird lime and littered with owl pellets. Little mounds of plaster lay here and there in powdery piles, fallen from the walls to expose green-tinged stone, or a lattice of laths like the bare bones of the house.

It was nothing like that now. The floors were scoured and spread with brightly coloured rugs. The panelling had all been hammered back, although it had been left a weathered silver with a faint powdering of green mould still showing here and there. The plaster had been hacked from the other walls, exposing the rugged grey stone from which the building had been constructed. A series of small rooms had been made into one big open space which stretched upwards and away under an upper-storey gallery. A wide wooden staircase had replaced the narrow, twisting stairs.

Despite the heat of the day outside, huge logs glowed and fell to ashes in the cavernous fireplace.

'These walls . . .' Lucia measured two hand spans. 'So thick! I find it cold in here even on a day as hot as this.' She rubbed her arms. 'That's why I like to keep a fire going. Thin blood, you see.'

The massive wooden beams running across the ceiling were festooned with garlands of feathery hops, sheaves of drying leaves, curling strips of bark, shrivelled bunches of seaweed tied next to dangling strings of onions and garlic. There were loops of what looked like little dried pixie hats strung with withered toadstools, thick and leathery like wizened ears.

Iron stands of various sizes stood on the stone-flagged floor. They held ranks of thick candles like fat stalagmites, ribbed with dripped wax. Richard imagined them all lit, soft light glinting on the brass lamps and incense burners hanging from the ceiling. The effect would be magical.

Exotic. That was the word. And strange. A vast oak dresser and open wooden cabinets mounted on the walls held odd groupings of objects: animal skulls; pearly translucent shells; a long curving polished horn cased in silver; carved wooden dolls; a smooth-faced stone figure with slitted eyes; fossils; flint arrows and a polished axe head. Blue and green ribbed glass bottles stood in a row in front of rust-pocked enamel adverts for long-forgotten remedies, brands of cigarettes, potted meats. It was like something out of a weird museum.

In every part of the room, the unusual and the ordinary stood next to each other: beaten copper pots piled on a bright red Aga cooker; an ironing board propped against a wooden carved wayside Madonna. A beautiful pottery bowl of the deepest blue-green held an array of foreign-looking fruits which were all going over to rot. The sun shone through panels of stained glass set into the windows and covered the floor with a moving pattern of red, green and blue. Richard was aware that he was gawking, but he couldn't help it. He had never been anywhere like this room in his life. As he stepped forward, he was walking though puddles of light.

In fact, the room was far more squalid than it looked at first sight. The long, low table in the centre was littered with bottles and overflowing ashtrays. Bright woven fabrics strewn over the furniture disguised dull red sagging moquette. A young man lay sprawled on a huge sofa. Richard had failed to notice him in his initial awe. He was pale-skinned and very thin, his black cotton shirt clinging close to his narrow chest. He wore purple velvet loon pants, stained with oil on the sides and threadbare on the thighs, slung low enough to show his jutting hip bones. His long bare feet stuck out from his frayed bell-bottoms and hung over the arm of the sofa. The toenails were black, the soles gritty and grey as asphalt. The young man ignored Richard and Lucia, rolling over to crush his cigarette out, stabbing it into the centre of an egg congealing on a plate on the floor. He reached for a square tobacco tin, took out a roll-up, lit the twisted end and inhaled deeply, closing his eyes, holding the smoke inside.

Lucia reached out and tapped the back of his hand. He held the roll-up towards her. The smoke curled in a thin coil, filling the room with a sharp pungent scent. Richard sniffed, it smelt like smouldering weeds on a bonfire, not like his mother's cigarettes.

'Thanks, Joe.' Lucia inhaled deeply like the boy, holding the smoke down in her chest. She let it out in a long stream, her eyes narrowed. 'Umm, that's good. Want some?' She held the roll-up out to Richard.

'Er, no.' He shook his head. 'I don't smoke, thanks.'

He'd only tried once or twice, and hadn't liked the taste.

23

Anyway, they were smoking pot. He was trying hard not to show his shock. That was not an ordinary cigarette.

'It's fantastic stuff. *Fantastic!* Well done, Joe.' She passed the joint back to the boy on the sofa. 'Joe, meet Ricardo. He's my new friend.'

'Hi.' Joe waved a long-fingered languid hand without looking at him.

'Would you like a drink?' Lucia skirted the heavy low table and picked carefully through the empties, trying not to disturb the ashtrays, lifting bottles one after another, tipping them to gauge the contents. 'There must be some in one of these.'

'I'm OK, thanks. Really.'

Richard's family drank wine only at Christmas and sometimes on special occasions. He couldn't imagine drinking it in the middle of an ordinary day.

'Are you sure?' Lucia's smooth brow wrinkled with sudden concern. 'It's so hot. You must have something!'

'I wouldn't mind some pop,' Richard said, not because he was really thirsty. More to please her than anything. 'If you have any.'

'Pop?' Lucia's brow wrinkled some more. 'I don't think we have any of that. Do we have pop, Joe?' The boy on the sofa seemed not to hear. 'Clio would know. What's the time?'

She looked round, suddenly uncertain, apprehensive even, reminding Richard of the White Rabbit in *Alice*. If she was searching for a clock Richard didn't see one, and neither she nor Joe wore a watch.

'A quarter past three,' he supplied, looking at his new digital timepiece.

'That's all right then!' Her face cleared. 'They should be finishing.' She went to the foot of the stairs. 'Darling?

24

Can you spare Clio? We have a guest and he's asking for pop.'

She made him sound about five years old. Richard cringed.

The girl was already coming down the stairs. She descended slowly, adjusting a wrap like Lucia's, tying it under her arm. Behind her came a man. He kept to the shadows but Richard could feel his presence, the way all their attention was focused on him. He was tall and dark, with a pointed beard streaked with silver and long black hair to his shoulders. He was thin, like Joe, but wore a loose flowing robe and thonged sandals on his bare bony feet. He looked like a prophet or someone from an older time. He stood, arms folded, staring from under jutting brows, studying the room below him, his black eyes fixed on the boy. Richard felt the stare and it made him uncomfortable. He was glad when Lucia spoke to introduce him.

'This is Ricardo.' Lucia rolled his name again, making it sound exotic. The girl grinned. No doubt at the contrast he presented. 'I found him in the garden. Now he wants pop.'

Richard studied the floor in embarrassment. When he glanced up, the man had gone.

'There's some lemonade in the larder,' the girl said, coming down the stairs towards him. 'Come with me.'

He drank quickly, gulping down the warm liquid. Most of the fizz had gone out of it. He was suddenly self-conscious now someone his own age was with him, someone wearing almost nothing. She wore a jewel in her nose, like Lucia. He'd never seen that before. He wondered what it felt like. Did it block up your nostril? Could you feel it there, like a bogey? How much did it hurt to have done? She had a mark on her bare arm, as though someone had held her there, printing her skin with paint. He looked away

25

from her, taking in the small room: an open cupboard by the door held packets of herbs and spices, rice and pasta, bottles of oil and jars with foreign labels. The other end of the room was different, more like an old-fashioned larder. Ranks of grimy old flagons stood under wide dusty shelves which held a scattering of rusted tins, unlabelled jam pots and baskets filled with dried-up shrivelled things. A small cobwebbed window in the middle of the back wall gave on to a formal-looking garden, little hedges surrounding groups of tall plants. It looked like a herb garden – he recognized the deep pink splashes of foxgloves and there were other plants, nearly as tall, some with thick furry leaves, others with purple-black nodding flowers.

'Have you finished?' She held her hand out for his glass.

He nodded, wiping his mouth on the back of his hand. He didn't like to stare, but he couldn't help it. Her eyes were such an unusual colour. Unusual and beautiful: the irises dark smoky violet, flecked with ash, ringed with black. Not that he got much of a chance to study them, because she would barely look at him. He found himself staring just in the hope that she would look back, but she kept her face turned away from him, so he studied her cheek, her face in profile. Her skin was the colour of dark honey and flawless. She must spend a lot of time out in the sun.

'Good.' She took the glass from him. 'Then you'd better be off.'

She walked towards the door, making it clear that he was to follow.

'Not going already?' Lucia looked up from the sofa where she was draped over Joe, sharing another joint with him. There was no sign of the older man. 'I thought that you might like to stay for supper. I've a tagine in the Aga.'

26

Even though Lucia didn't bother herself with the more mundane aspects of housework, she was a very good cook.

'No, Luce. He has to go now,' the girl answered for him. She sounded cold, indifferent, superior. 'Don't you?'

Richard nodded. He wouldn't stay where he wasn't wanted and this girl had made her feelings pretty clear on that point. Besides that, he didn't even know what a tagine was, let alone whether he would like it or not. Although it smelt all right.

'Never mind. Some other time.' Lucia smiled at him. She was as warm as her daughter was frosty. 'You know where we are, so don't be a stranger. You're welcome any time. Isn't he, Clio? Joe?'

Neither of them replied to her. The girl escorted him back out into the garden. He stood blinking in the sunlight, blinded after the smoky darkness inside. It was like waking to another world.

'Well, Rickrickyrichard, it's been nice meeting you. I'll make sure next time that we've got some pop.'

She gave a laugh that seemed to imply that there wouldn't be a next time and gripped his arm in a painful squeeze, just above the elbow, propelling him across the lawn. When they got to the steps, she gave a quick backwards glance, up towards the house. There was nothing to see, the windows were as blank as reflecting mirrors, but he had a feeling that they were being watched.

'You look like a nice boy,' she said, holding his arm even tighter, leaning close to whisper in his ear. 'So I'm offering some advice. *Don't* come back.'

Her sharp pinching made his eyes water; her hostility hurt even more. At that moment, she didn't have to worry, he had no intention of coming back. Nevertheless, as he went down the steps he felt in some way cast out and bereft; as if a prize he'd just been awarded had been suddenly snatched away from him, impossible to get back, which only made him want it more. He ran off without another word to her, nursing an ache inside him that had not been there before.

He might never have gone back, stayed right out of their lives, if it hadn't been for Dylan. But if it hadn't been for Dylan, he'd never have gone up to the Wish House in the first place. Strange how things work out.

Dylan had been his friend ever since they had started coming down here on holiday, when Richard was nine and Dylan was going on eleven. His dad owned the caravan site, it was on his land, and the first thing Richard did when he came down on holiday was go and find Dylan. They were inseparable, playing together every day, camping out at night, in the fields, in the woods, on the dunes. If it was raining they would sleep in the hayloft in one of the barns. Richard loved those nights, settling down next to Dylan with the straw prickling through their blankets, talking in low whispers as though they might disturb the animals in their stalls. The rich pungent smell drifting up from them turned from stomach-wrenching to comforting as the rain drummed on the V-shaped roof and the soothing sounds of shuffling, lowing, snuffling and munching drifted up with the warmth from the animals below.

This time things would be different. As soon as the car was unpacked Richard had set off to find Dylan, leaving his parents to air the 'van and set up for their stay. They hadn't been down since last year, but always came for a month in the summer.

'He's working with his dad,' Dylan's mum had said when Richard went to call him.

She was hosing down the yard, directing the jet down at the ground just long enough to exchange a few words. Her baggy brown overalls belonged to Dylan's dad. She wore them cinched in at the waist with one of his thick leather belts. She blew a corkscrew strand of springy brown hair out of her eyes as she studied Richard, her mouth compressed to a straight line. Her pale blue eyes narrowed with what seemed to him like contempt. *He won't be playing out with* you *any more, sunshine*, her look seemed to say before she turned away. *He's a man now.* She was a woman of few words and didn't take nonsense. She directed the hose up and out again, not prepared to waste any more on Richard. Some of the spray caught him on the legs.

Richard had mumbled something and gone off alone, left on his own, at a loose end. That's how he'd ended up going to the Wish House.

Rounding the next corner on his way back to the caravan site, Richard found the road blocked by the herd of cows. They filled the whole width of it, jostling and pushing at each other, lowing in complaint at the constraining narrowness of the lane. A black and white sheepdog ranged at their heels, snapping and plunging to keep the bumbling beasts going forward, and a boy yipped and called, tapping their glossy black backs with a stick.

'Hey, Dylan!' Richard shouted above the din of the cattle. 'Wait up! Wait for me!'

The boy turned and called back a greeting, waving his stick in salutation. He waited for Richard to catch up with him and they went on together. Dylan looked different. Older. He had grown his curly black hair longer, his chin showed dark stubble and sideburns edged down his jaw. He was taller, broader in the chest and shoulders. His body was lean and tanned from working outside all day. He was shirtless at the moment and a line of dark hair snaked up to his navel, which lay coiled in a cleft between tightly packed muscles that had not been there before.

'Working for my dad full time now I've left school.'

'You've left!' Richard was shocked.

'I'll only end up here.' Dylan looked away from him, out to the fields that sloped gently down to the sea. 'So what's the point of going on and sitting more exams? Dad says college is a waste of time.' He turned back, squinting down at Richard. 'What you been up to, anyway?'

'I haven't done O levels yet –'

'Not that!' Dylan laughed. 'I meant today, you pillock!'

'Oh.' Richard grinned back. 'I went up to the Wish House.'

'That artist's up there now.'

'I know. They invited me in.'

'Oh, yeah?' Dylan paused to pluck a stalk of grass to chew, prepared to be interested. 'What they like?'

'I dunno.' Richard shrugged. He couldn't put into words what he thought, even to himself. 'A bit weird, I suppose.'

'That's what they say. Right bunch of weirdos. Old-style hippies. Free love, drugs – anything goes. You see that?'

'They were smoking pot,' Richard offered.

'Pot?' Dylan blew out his cheeks in disgust. 'That all? Everyone smokes that.'

'Have you tried it?'

'Sure.' Dylan squinted down at him. 'Course. Everyone has. Haven't you?'

'Well, kind of . . .' Richard lied.

'Anyway, that's not what I'm talking about. They do

30

other stuff. Weird stuff. LSD, magic mushrooms – you name it. They walk around with no clothes on, down on the beach and all. Ma's helping get a petition going in the village. Not popular with the caravanners, and the beach is a public area. They treat their end like it's private. About the free love –' he dropped his voice a little bit and came closer to Richard, as if concerned that the cows should not overhear him – 'it's true. I know some of the boys who did work on the house. She puts it about a bit. The old man couldn't care less.'

'Who? The girl?'

'Not her, man! I meant the mother!'

'I expected the place to be deserted.' Richard smiled. 'Had a bit of a surprise when I got up there. She was stretched out on the lawn . . .' He paused before letting the last word out: 'starkers.'

Dylan whistled in a mix of envy and appreciation.

'Lucky bastard! Wish I'd seen that! I've heard she's not bad. For her age, like. The old man, the artist, he owns the house, been in his family a long time. His dad used to entertain there. Artists and poets. Famous in their day. The place was notorious. My gran's full of stories. When the old man died, his son took over. Used to come down every summer, but that was years ago now.' The cows had stopped to graze the steep sides of the lane. Dylan used his stick to urge them on. 'Been living away. Left the place to go derelict. We were hoping to buy it; convert it into holiday lets. Then we heard they were coming back.'

Dylan shook his head as if he found it hard to understand why.

'How long they been back, then?' Richard asked.

He wanted to know more about the family in the Wish

House. Not that he'd be going there, not after the girl threw him out, but he couldn't help being curious.

'Since last autumn. They had it all done out. Spent a bomb on it. Boys from the village done most of the work.' Dylan laughed. 'Same ones who'd been robbing the place out. Kept 'em busy for months. Joe – the son – the dipstick in the loon pants? He was in charge of the work.'

'He's her *son*?' Richard was surprised by that.

'Yes. What did you think?'

Richard shrugged. 'I don't know.'

'Think she doesn't look old enough?' Dylan asked eagerly.

Richard shrugged again. 'I guess.'

It wasn't that. It was the way she was all over him. The way they shared a joint. Their *easiness* together. Didn't seem right in mother and son. Not in his experience. He didn't know anyone else who behaved like that around their mother. But he wasn't going to say that to Dylan who might sneer as though that was how really cool people behaved. Although he couldn't quite see Dylan with *his* ma . . .

'What are you grinning about?' Dylan gave him a curious look.

Richard shook his head.

'OK, then. About Joe. More useful than he looks. He's all right, as a matter of fact.' Dylan laughed, picking up the thread. 'He was at some posh school and got thrown out, but he's been to college. Good with electrics, sorted the jukebox out in the pub. Buys his round, no problem.'

Dylan probably spent most nights down the pub now. He yipped at the cows and whistled to his dog while Richard pulled some grass to chew. He wanted to ask about the girl, but didn't want Dylan to think he was interested.

Before he could make up his mind to do it, they were at the farm gate.

Dylan drove the cattle through, then turned to Richard.

'Got to milk this lot now.' He paused. 'Me and the boys will be in the pub later. I'd ask you down, but we'll be in the bar, like.'

Richard knew what Dylan was getting at. He looked too young. Even if he got in, they would never serve him.

'That's OK.' Richard took a step back. 'See you around, Dylan.'

'Yeah.' The older boy grinned. 'Nice to see you down.'

He went off, driving the cows into the milking parlour. Dylan was as friendly and affable as ever, but Richard had lost his childhood companion. They would not be spending this summer together. Things had changed. All that Richard could do now was go back to the caravan.

He walked past the little shop and the toilet block, then wove his way through the rows of vans, dodging washing lines, dads juggling TV aerials and hordes of children being called in for their tea. He'd be sent to get water from the standpipe when he got back. That was one of his jobs, along with carting rubbish, and emptying the plastic waste-water bucket which was always brimming and hard to carry without the scummy, greasy contents slopping against his legs. His dad would have been out fishing all day, and his mum would have been doing nothing. She didn't come on holiday to do chores. That's what she said.

She didn't cook much, either, just sat inside the van playing patience, or outside on one of the fold-up chairs, smoking and reading one of her detective novels. So it would be corned beef sandwiches for supper, unless his father had caught something. He'd made a little barbecue built up on bricks and would cook whatever he caught, no matter how inedible the fish. So the choice would be corned beef sandwiches; or oily blackened mackerel; or some nameless thing, all bones and skin. Richard's stomach turned at the thought of it.

After Richard had done his chores, they sat round the wood-effect Formica fold-out table, eating their meal off the green plastic caravan plates, washed down with milky tea out of matching cups. Dad hadn't caught anything, so it was corned beef.

Richard wondered what tagine was. It had smelt really good, rich and fragrant. He wondered what it tasted like. Better than anything he'd ever had, he was willing to bet. Even given her aversion to garlic and anything foreign, his mother was not much of a cook. He imagined dining by candlelight, eating delicious food, aromatic with herbs and spices, drinking red wine out of crystal glasses while Lucia bent over the table to serve him, her lips smiling, her wrap falling open . . .

'We're going down the pub,' his mother announced.

'What?'

'I said, we're going down the pub. Why do I always have to say everything twice?'

'Oh.' Richard heard her this time. 'Oh, right.'

'Well?' His mother rolled her eyes with impatience. 'Do you want to come, or not? We can sit out in the garden. It's a fine night.'

Sitting at a picnic table, drinking ginger beer with his mum and dad. That really would put the tin lid on it.

'No, thanks, Mum,' Richard replied. 'I'll stay here, if you don't mind. I'll be all right.'

'Suit yourself.' His mother clicked open her handbag, extracting lipstick and compact. 'Do the washing-up then, there's a good lad. And see if you can get the telly working.'

It was hard to hear what she was saying through the contorted O-shape her mouth took on as she applied her lipstick. 'Dad can't get a picture.'

Forest of Celyddon: Druids' Copse

(1966) Oil on panel
29.2 x 23.5 cm
National Library of Wales
Jethro Arnold Dalton R.A. (1916–1976)

J. A. Dalton painted these woods obsessively from when he was a boy. In a radio interview given in 1966 he described them as: 'The sacred grove. Beautiful, mysterious, a place where legend and folklore come together. Impossibly ancient, Arawn, King of Annwn, the Celtic underworld, is said to have hunted with his hounds in these very woods. [Pause] There is supposed to be a valley near there, a lost valley: the Vale of Illusion, the Realm of Glamour. A remnant of the weird land where the gods of old still walk: Hafgan Summer-White and Arawn Silver-Tongue. [Laughs] I've spent a lifetime looking, but I've yet to find it.'

(Taken from article 'Dalton Country', New Arts Review, 16 April 1968)

Richard couldn't get the telly to work either. He fiddled with the portable aerial but the picture slid about. It was like watching through falling ash. The reception was not much better on the radio – every time a song he liked came on the sound was swallowed by crackling static. He decided to go out while there was still some light. His parents wouldn't be back until closing time and he'd often wandered the hills with Dylan at night, so he knew the area pretty well and there was no danger of getting lost.

He took the path away from the cliffs and the sea, leaving the caravan park far behind until the little roofs looked like so many silver-backed playing cards set out for one of his mother's endless games of patience.

He walked with no sense of destination, letting his feet take him wherever, following animal tracks, this path and then that through the waist-high bracken, not caring that he walked alone. There was no one to see him and wonder at his lack of companions. He was gripped by a sense of adventure for the first time that summer. This was his favourite place to be.

His way took him over low hills and down into shadowed vales. The land buckled behind him in gentle folds. He paused to look back, to see how far he had come. The sea was some distance now, shining in the last of the sun, a bright triangle of beaten silver between interlocking fingers of green-mantled hills. In front of him stood the dark line of Celyddon Wood. The trees cloaked rising ground, draping round it, one hem dipping to the deep valley bottom where a little river showed like a ribbon of steel.

The sun had all but gone from the hills, but the night still held some of the glimmer of midsummer. Richard stood for a moment, the hairs prickling on the back of his neck, rising like fur on his arms although he was in no way cold. Above him, the thin white blade of a moon had appeared, sharp as a scalpel in the deepening blue of the sky and far away a few bright stars dotted the shadowy purple horizon, shining out like distant lamps. He turned and took the path into the high trees. The leaves seemed to stir all around him as he entered the wood, letting out a rustling, whooshing sound, as if the forest breathed, welcoming him into the mossy gloom of its dim interior.

He followed wide ridings and winding leaf-strewn paths, heading for a special place he'd found with Dylan years ago, deep in the secret centre of the wood. At some point in the past part of the land must have slipped away, leaving a wide hollow above a steep valley. A grove of hanging oaks squatted like a coven, branches bent over the place. One of the trees stood right on the edge of the precipice. Massive roots, clotted with red earth, jutted out in a thick tangled mass and made an excellent roof for the hidden area beneath, keeping the floor of it as dry as a cave. Layers of fallen leaves, the litter of many years, made a thick, soft golden carpet. They had camped out there some nights, spreading their blankets on beds of springy dry bracken, sleeping under the whispering trees, with the stars shining though the shifting leaves.

They were both mad on Tolkien and would pretend to be in *The Lord of the Rings*, sleeping out like Frodo and the Company. Richard would be Frodo. Dylan didn't like the idea of being a hobbit, so he was always Aragorn or

Boromir. On other occasions they would pretend to be hunters, or warriors of ancient times who had once roamed these forests. In some parts of the wood the trees were really old, the gnarled trunks grey and green, crusted with lichen. They grew low to the ground, the branches spread out like the grappling fingers of upturned hands. Those places had a strange, spooky quality. Sometimes you couldn't even find these groves again, that was the weird thing. And when you did, you could actually imagine that you had wandered into a different time. That you would come stumbling out to find that the world you knew had changed, left you behind.

It was easy to imagine all sorts of things and it had been good fun. Richard followed the path through tall smooth-barked beeches and rough oak trees; all the time the leaves whispered his memories. He could feel rising within him the excitement of those nights spent out in the open watching the red glow of a fire in the deep dark of the night. Then waking in the early morning with the bottom of the valley lost in layers of white mist, waiting while Dylan got the billycan bubbling, and then drinking the black bitter brew sweetened with sugar brought in a twist of paper. They told each other that tea had never, ever tasted so good. This was true adventure. Like you read about in books.

The path branched and divided but he thought that he remembered the way. Further into the wood the track narrowed, brambles encroached and nettles grew tall. Richard stopped and cut a switch from a hazel bush to beat back the vegetation. His imagination took over as he slashed and hacked a way through the undergrowth. He could almost hear the whack of arrows, the thudding hoofs of pursuing horsemen. He made a break for it and ran on, fighting off enemies all the way to the hollow. If anyone else had been there he wouldn't have done it. To behave this way, to lose himself in play, would seem silly. Childish. But no one was here, so who was to know?

They were close now. He could hear the undergrowth parting; the wickering, snorting of their horses as they paced towards him. He was breathing heavily himself. Sweat burned in grazes and scratches he didn't even know he had. He stood for a moment, disconcerted. The wood was suddenly very quiet. His own breathing was the only sound he could hear. The ground around him looked alien and unfamiliar, even though this was territory that he thought he knew. Maybe he'd come to an unexplored part, although he could have sworn that he'd already been everywhere with Dylan. He was looking for the great oak tree and sanctuary but the light was leaving the wood, night pooling between the trees. Things looked different.

He started off again quiet and cautious, listening for the faint jingle of bridle bells, the fine soft ringing of spurs. He crept on, keeping low. Suddenly, a great fallen trunk blocked his way, the dead branches stretched out like a hand pointing towards rising ground where the trees grew taller. He knew where he was. He gave one last defiant whoop and made for the sheltering grove. He reached the tallest oak, grasped one of the thick roots at its base and swung himself down into his hiding place. They would never find him now.

The girl started back, as surprised as he was, drawing herself up and shrinking away like a startled faun. He hung, dangling, staring at her in amazement, wishing the film would run backwards and flip him out of there.

'Sorry,' he said, dropping down eventually. 'Didn't mean to scare you. I didn't expect anyone to be here.'

'You didn't scare me.' Her reply was haughty. 'I didn't

expect anyone to come crashing in like a drunken gorilla, that's all.'

She obviously meant for him to leave, but Richard didn't see why he should. It was as much his place as hers, that's how he saw it. He didn't think it odd that they should both end up in the same place together. Not then. He just plonked himself down, putting a careful distance between them, and sat there hugging his knees. She ignored him and they both stared out into the last of the light, watching the swifts and swallows screaming and dipping in weaving flight above the descending valley, skimming insects from the deepening blue.

An owl flew out and all the small birds scattered. The hunter made no cry, but it was suddenly quiet enough to hear the soft thud of its beating wings.

'This place is special,' she said. Her voice was husky and had lost its hostility. She spoke quietly, almost in a whisper, as if she accepted him here.

'I know,' he replied. 'It's special to me, too.'

'I used to come here with Jay. He used to tell me stories.'

'Who's Jay?'

'You know.' But Richard didn't. 'You saw him this afternoon.'

'The boy with the dirty feet?'

'Not him!' She looked at Richard as if he was imbecilic. 'That's Joe.'

'Oh! You mean the artist?'

'Yes. I used to come here with him. He's my father.'

'Oh,' he leaned forward, trying to see her face better. 'When was that?'

'When I was little.' She bent her head. Her long black hair fell like a heavy curtain. She reached out her hand, stirring the dry leaves about her feet. 'When we lived here before. A long time ago.'

'I used to come here with my friend Dylan.' Richard leaned back, resting on his elbows. 'We used to camp out here. We used to tell stories, too.'

'Is Dylan the boy who lives at the farm?'

Richard nodded. 'Do you know him?'

She didn't answer that. She turned to him, pushing the weight of her hair back behind her ear.

'What were your stories about?'

'Well, um . . .'

Richard was reluctant to tell her, sure that she would think they were silly, afraid that she was drawing him out so that she could mock him further. If that was her intention, she showed no sign of it. The antagonism that she'd shown earlier seemed to have disappeared and she sat quiet, waiting, her smudged violet eyes fixed on him. He was struck again by their beauty and kept wanting to see them more closely, just to confirm that they were really that shade.

'Just stupid boys' stuff,' he went on eventually. 'You know?'

'No.' She shook her head. 'I don't know many boys. Except Joe, and he's my brother, and older. So he doesn't count. Tell me about Dylan and the stories.'

'I don't know. It seems daft now.' Richard really didn't want to tell her, certain that she would laugh. 'Promise you won't take the piss?'

'I promise.' She nodded, serious-faced, and crossed her heart.

'We used to pretend we were in adventures.' The words came out in a rush. '*The Lord of the Rings*, the Knights of King Arthur. That kind of stuff. We used to camp out.' He looked around. 'Spend the night here.'

'Really? How exciting!'

He looked at her sharply. She had to be taking the piss, whatever she had promised. She had been so superior at the house, so dismissive, and she hadn't exactly welcomed him dropping in just a short while ago. But now she seemed genuinely interested. Either she was truly mercurial, or as lonely as he was. Perhaps both. He frowned. Or maybe there was something else going on here, something he didn't understand.

'Yeah.' Richard glanced around. 'We found an old ammunition box with stuff in it hidden up there.' He indicated a recess under the jutting roots of the big oak tree. 'There was a little frying pan and an old billycan, a couple of blankets, some candle stubs and matches that had gone all soft. We got new candles. The blankets were all damp with mildew and eaten up by moths, so we brought our own up here.'

He crawled to the back of the overhang, digging in the piles of accumulated leaves. He came back lugging a battered tin box.

'Look.'

It was still there.

Dylan had put a padlock on it. Richard used a stone to smash off the rusty hasp. A strong smell of damp came from a mildewed blanket. Beneath it were a few candle stubs, the blackened billycan, a battered skillet, a couple of tin plates and two tin cups. At the bottom was a pot of Hartley's, the jam gone over to black slime coated with a thick bumpy layer of blue-green mould.

Clio peered as if into a treasure chest.

'How absolutely brilliant! Just like you said! It's like the Famous Five, or *Swallows and Amazons*! They camped out all the time. I used to *love* those books!'

'Well, yes.' Richard sat back on his heels. 'I guess . . .'

Richard and Dylan had always gone for fantasy with lots of fighting. Her particular choices had not been in their minds.

'We could do that.' She caught her lower lip between her teeth, her violet eyes on him. They looked dark now, almost black. 'We could camp out . . .'

The light was nearly gone. Her face had become a pale blur in the darkness, a white smudge. She leaned close to see him better, then closer still. He could feel the warmth from her skin. Her eyes closed, dark lashes sweeping down on to her cheeks. Her lips were very near, slightly parted, her breath came faster, smelling of sugared almonds, warm bread. She hesitated for just a moment, then put her hand on the back of his neck, pulling him towards her. There was no bumping of noses, or clashing of teeth, no clumsy angles as there had been with other girls. She spread her fingers up into his hair, guiding his face to hers. The kiss was soft, gentle and long. He felt her mouth open and her tongue was warm in his mouth. He'd never been kissed like this before. It took his breath from him. At last, she broke away.

'I said, we could camp out.' Her voice was deeper, roughened by her breathing.

'All right,' he replied.

Something seemed to melt and fall away deep within him and the words seemed to echo inside his head, reverberating through him, like a great wind roaring through the woods. He was in the grip of a greater excitement than he had ever known in his life. It spread through him, arcing back and forth like static, tingling down to his fingers and toes. It was a feeling entirely new to him. She kissed him again, pulling him down to lie beside her, her mouth

46

slippery on his. She seemed so sure about what to do. It did not occur to him until sometime afterwards to wonder exactly how she knew.

Eventually she pulled away from him and sat up adjusting her clothing.

'I think we better go soon. Before we do, though, I think we should make a list . . .'

She took a black notebook from her pocket. The pages were thick cream-coloured cartridge paper. It was secured by a rubber band. The book was fat with things slipped and slotted in between the pages: pictures, postcards, pressed flowers. She flicked through to find a blank page. He glimpsed sketches and accompanying lines of writing in a big, bold italic hand.

'You should always carry a notebook. That's what Jay says. Never know when it might come in useful. Now, what will we need?'

'Need for what?'

'Camping out.'

She sat cross-legged, writing out her list with a thick-leaded pencil. They hadn't gone all the way, but they'd not been far off it. Richard rose up on his elbows. What kind of girl would want to make lists right now? He wasn't sufficiently savvy about girls to know if it was just her, or if that's how they all were.

'Here.' She tore the page out with a crack. Richard almost winced. It seemed a shame to spoil a book like that. 'This is what you have to bring.' She folded the page and then leaned over to tuck the note into his pocket. 'We'll meet here tomorrow night.' Her hand slid down, parting his unbuttoned shirt. 'It's getting awfully dark,' she whispered, 'but I have a torch. I don't think we have to go just yet, do you?'

Head of Chwyfleian
Study for: Chwyfleian Prophecies, She Tells a Tale

(1975) Gouache on paper

76.2 cm x 50.8 cm

Tribereth Gallery

Jethro Arnold Dalton R.A. (1916–1976)

'According to legend, Myrddin lost his reason and retreated to the forest of Celyddon to live with the wild ones. Here he meets Chwyfleian, a young prophetess.' In the painting, *Chwyfleian Prophecies* . . . Dalton combines his long fascination both with Celtic legend and the Pre-Raphaelite School of painters. His positioning of Myrddin (Merlin) and the young prophetess recall Edward Burne-Jones's *The Beguiling of Merlin*, as does this exquisite gouache study, right down to the angle of the gaze and the garland of snakes in the model's hair. The model for this study, and for the painting, was his daughter and 'junior muse', Clio Dalton.

Dalton comments: 'I was drawn to the idea of the ensnaring enchantress, the spell-binding power of youth and beauty. I've always admired the Burne-Jones painting, and think he captures the moment of enchantment. The transfer of power from one to the other – it's almost palpable. I wanted to capture some of that feeling here.'

(Exhibition notes: Tribereth Gallery – Dalton retrospective, 1980)

He was camping out with Dylan. That's what he would tell them. What if they saw Dylan at the pub? His mother didn't fuss much about what he did, but she disliked the illogical and had an instinct for stories that didn't add up. He'd say they were meeting after. But what if Dylan was too pissed to go anywhere much? He'd think of something.

Richard went through his cover story, hunting and chasing down all the possible problems and eventualities. In the end he didn't have to worry. Not for that night, anyway. His parents decided on a quiet night in. Dad had even managed to get a tolerable picture on the telly.

He packed his rucksack with the stuff on her list that he'd bought from the shop and set out just as the evening was falling. He'd spent all day in a heightened state, worrying about his story, oscillating between towering excitement and growing terror. He had almost no experience with girls. Last night, he'd gone way further than ever before. Further, he suspected, than any of his friends at school, no matter what they said. She didn't seem to have any inhibitions at all. Tonight she would expect more. How would he know what to do?

He knew the mechanics, but sensed there was a gap between theory and practice. What if he couldn't perform? What if he came too soon? What if he *thought* she wanted to, but she actually didn't? How would he know? He went over in his mind all the things he'd read, all the things he'd heard at school, but he could recall . . . nothing. His thoughts fractured and fled away, leaving him with a terrifying blankness. There was no one to ask here, even in a roundabout way, not like at school. He could not exactly ask Dad, and Dylan was out.

He'd even thought of going on the bus to the nearest town and trying to buy a book – *The Joy of Sex* or something like that – or even going to the library. He could memorize the relevant passages, maybe take notes. But what if Mum wanted to go with him? Or, even worse, offered to take him? Or suggested to Dad that they all go as a family outing? He came out in a cold sweat just thinking about it.

And what would he do about protection? The 'necessary', as his friend Giles called it. Giles had advised him: always carry a pack of three in your wallet. As Giles himself did. He'd held out a palmful of creased and bent silver foil squares, in case Richard did not believe him.

There was a machine in the Gents at the camp. Richard waited until no one was about and went to check it out. It just took his money. When he turned the handle nothing came out. He'd given it a good thump just as some old bloke had come in telling him, 'Steady on! That's someone else's property!' Adding, 'Shouldn't be needing them things at your age,' before disappearing into one of the cubicles. So he'd come out fifty pence the lighter with nothing to show for it.

He had vague thoughts about chemist shops and barbers, but that would mean going to Tenby or Carmarthen, which was out of the question. Anyway, he would be too embarrassed.

In the end he didn't do anything.

By the time he got to the woods, he was almost hoping that she wouldn't be there, that she wouldn't show up, but as he swung down from the tree root, there she was. She smiled at him. He'd never seen anyone so beautiful. Just the sight of her brought all his fears rushing back. This had to be a mistake. How could she be waiting for him? He wanted to save her the disappointment by flipping himself back out of there and disappearing forever.

'Well?' Her smile widened. 'Are you going to hang around there all night?'

He let himself down and approached cautiously, keeping his distance so she couldn't see how he was shaking, how nervous he was.

She had been busy collecting dry bracken, forming it into a springy mattress under one of several bright striped blankets that she had brought with her. He unpacked his rucksack, showing her what he'd managed to collect, setting out what they would need, stowing the rest in the old ammunition box. Gradually he relaxed. If they did practical things, like setting up camp, then maybe nothing else would happen.

'You know, today –' she said, sitting back on her heels – 'I couldn't stop thinking how strange it was that we both ended up in the same place last night, without either of us knowing the other was coming here.'

'I suppose.' Richard shrugged. It *was* a bit weird when you came to think. Very weird. Not that he'd spent too much time pondering on it. He'd had other things on his mind. 'Just coincidence, I guess.'

'You could call it that.' Clio frowned. 'Lucia calls it synchronicity.'

'What's that?'

'It's quite hard to explain. It's like if I said a word, and at the same time you were thinking the exact same thing. Or if I was thinking about you, and the next thing you're there. With me. Like a summoning.'

'Were you? Thinking about me?'

'Well, no.' Clio glanced away quickly. 'But for both of us to end up here, neither of us knowing, that's more than coincidence. That's what Lucia says. She says it was meant to be.' She picked up a dried leaf and examined the veins on the back of it. 'She reads tarot cards. She knows about stuff like that. She has a crystal ball wrapped in black velvet.'

'You *told* her?'

'Of course.' Her brow cleared. 'What's wrong with that?'

'Nothing.' Richard shook his head. He just couldn't imagine discussing anything like that with either of his parents. It was private. Not their business. Beneath their interest.

'She read the tarot for me.'

'Oh yeah? What did it say?'

'Hmm.' The little frown was back again. 'It wasn't quite clear, but you were there: the Knave of Batons. He's never been in my spread before.' She hugged her knees and looked round. 'Chanterelles used to grow here.'

'What?' Her mind jumped quickly from one thing to another. Richard had trouble following her.

'Chanterelles. They're a kind of mushroom. Jay and I used to come here to pick them. It's a bit early yet.' She crawled to a corner of the overhang, hunting in the damp earth beneath the great tree roots. 'There's a little group here. Come and see.'

Richard crawled over, immediately recoiling from the orange-coloured fungi all clumped together like a writhing mass of knotted fingers.

'Ugh! They're toadstools! You don't eat them!'

'These aren't toadstools!' She laughed. '*Those* are toadstools!' She pointed up the bank to some sickly greenish-white caps poking through the leaf litter. 'And those.' She pointed to another clump, red and spotted, like something out of a fairy story. '*These* are perfectly edible. Delicious, in fact.' She gently stroked the blind heads, bruising the tender flesh, releasing a soft apricot scent. 'Jay's a real glutton for them.'

'Why don't you pick some for him?'

'There aren't enough here. We'll leave them to grow bigger. Oh, look. Magic mushrooms!'

Richard peered at the cluster of fawn-coloured fungi growing on a rotting stump. The bell-like caps, little hats on delicate, slender stems, trembled against her palm. They looked like any other toadstool to him. He couldn't see anything particularly magical about them.

'I'll have to tell Joe about these,' she said, wiping her hands on her jeans. 'He will be pleased.'

The hollow they were in faced due west and still retained some of the day's heat. They sat on the makeshift bed, staring out at the sunset.

As the day waned, mist had come creeping up the valley. The last rays of the sun transformed it into a golden river. Far away, you could see the summits of hills and further hills stretching into the milky distance, and nearer the tops of the trees showed like islands through the gilded fog. The familiar was obscured and they seemed to be looking out at some other-worldly landscape, a magical, mysterious place where anything was possible. They stared out for a long time, neither of them speaking, until Richard did not know how to break the silence between them.

'Jay says that there is a valley near here, a lost valley – the Vale of Illusion, he calls it,' she said at last. 'It is the Realm of Glamour, where the gods of old still walk: Hafgan Summer-White and Arawn Silver-Tongue. It must

T040713

be near, because Arawn is said to hunt with his hounds in these very woods; sometimes people hear them yelling.'

Richard nodded. On an evening like this, such things seemed just about possible. Dylan had told him legends about this place. They had woven them into their games.

'Merlin, too.' Clio turned towards him. 'He's supposed to be here with the white phantom, Chwyfleian, lost forever in his own enchantment. Do you think it could be true?'

She caught her lower lip between her teeth in that way she had and leaned towards him, her violet eyes looking into his.

'I don't know . . .' Richard said, his voice thick.

His heart was beating hard. He could think of nothing to say. Words seemed clotted in his chest. Instead, he put his arms around her and pulled her to him, astonished at himself, proud that he had taken the initiative.

He woke in the chill of the early morning to find her staring down at him.

'You are so beautiful,' she said, running the back of her hand over his chest. 'No wonder . . .'

'No wonder what?'

'Oh, nothing.'

Richard shook his head. He didn't think of himself as beautiful. It was a term reserved for girls. For girls like her. He propped himself on his elbows, happy just to look. *She* was certainly beautiful. Half hidden by her black hair, lithe and slender, small breasted, pale in the very early morning light. He had never seen anything so lovely. He thought that he would never get over her. Desire and longing would ache inside him forever, like a wound that could never heal.

'I really don't understand. I mean, back at the Wish House, when I first saw you . . .'

'What about it?'

'Well, you weren't very friendly. But now . . .'

'Exactly! *That's* synchronicity!'

She announced the word triumphantly, as if it explained everything, making any further speculation as to why her feelings might have changed towards him entirely unnecessary. Her initial hostility had been based on intuition. Her hand went to her upper arm, her fingers fitting themselves to the bracelet of bruises as she tried to explain it to him. She'd had a feeling, a very strong feeling, that he was bringing trouble to them. But first impressions can be wrong. Lucia hadn't thought so at all. And in such things Clio deferred to her.

'And Jay . . .' she started to say.

'Jay what?' Richard asked, suddenly apprehensive. What if she'd told him, too?

She shook her head. 'We have synchronicity. That's what matters.'

'How did you get those?' Richard asked, touching the patches of yellow and purple.

She held her left arm out for inspection.

'Pretty colours, don't you think? Violet and cadmium yellow.'

His fingers travelled to her shoulders, tracing along the delicate collarbone to the hollow below her throat and then moved on and down to her breasts. She shivered and fell towards him, pulling the blanket over them both. Her skin was cool against his, a slightly chill mushroom dampness; her slippery hair smelt of smoke and leaf mould, the spirit of the earth. The smell of either thing would always bring him back here again. When they first made love she'd cried out. He had worried that he was hurting her in some way, but now he was growing used to that. She was as uninhibited in her pleasure as she was in everything else. There was no one to hear them. Her cries fitted the wildness of the place, like a vixen or some other creature of the night. He felt pride, but also a kind of fear, knowing that he could bring her such strange pleasure.

They were as wild as each other. They made love until the sun was full up and they were both exhausted.

He lay next to her, thinking how he'd spent the previous day worrying, laughing at how foolish he'd been.

'What's so funny?' She dropped a shower of leaves over him.

'Nothing,' he said. 'Just happy, that's all.'

He had not needed condoms. Clio had been on the pill since she started her periods. Lucia had Joe when she was very young and didn't want her daughter to be caught in the same way.

'Who was the father?' Richard asked

'Jay, of course.' Clio looked surprised at the question. 'He took her to Italy. They were married there. That's where she changed her name to Lucia. My grandparents looked after Joe when he was young.'

'Didn't they mind?'

'Mind what?'

'Well, you said she was very young. He must have been much older . . .'

The parents of the girls Richard knew would have gone absolutely spare.

'They were friends with Jay and Meg.'

'Who's Meg?'

'Jay's first wife.' Clio smiled. 'She's coming down next weekend with Naeve and Freya.'

'Who are they?' Richard frowned, confused by all these new names.

'My half-sisters. They are much older than me. You'll like them. And Meg . . . she was friends with my grandmother, they were at school together. My grandparents are artists. They all lived in a community. It gets a bit complicated . . .'

'I bet.' Richard couldn't think what else to say. He couldn't get his head round it. Her life, what she accepted as normal, was so different. It made him feel even more deeply ordinary than he had before.

She seemed to sense how strange he found it and changed the subject.

'Don't worry about it. I'm hungry. Let's have some breakfast.'

After all that she still wanted to play at *Swallows and Amazons*. Richard set about getting a fire going and laughed.

There was a stream down in the valley with some deepish pools where the water fell in a series of boulder-strewn steps. The pools were not wide enough for swimming, but plenty deep enough for bathing. The dark brown peaty water was freezing, but neither of them minded. They splashed about, laughing and screaming, chasing each other, slipping and sliding over the slimy river stones until they became caught in another embrace, clinging on to each other, as cold and slippery as fish.

The sun had cleared the tops of the trees and was warming the valley floor. They lay drying, letting the sun warm them, before climbing back up to their eyrie. It was approaching noon. Clio said she had to get back.

'Why?'

'I've got things to do,' she replied, buttoning her shirt. 'You should, too. Won't your parents miss you?'

'I suppose,' he muttered reluctantly. He didn't want this ever to end.

'What's the problem?' She grabbed his chin, forcing him to look at her. 'We can meet back here. Same time as last night.'

'Why not earlier?' Richard was disappointed. The hours between now and then stretched away in a bleak expanse of time, impossible to fill.

'Told you. Things to do.' She kissed him lightly on the lips. 'See you later. I promise.'

She licked her finger and crossed her heart, then swung herself out of the place and was gone. Richard waited a while before following her. He did not know what he would do with his time before he could be here again. She had only been gone a few minutes, but it seemed like a lifetime to him.

The Chronicles of Pryderi

(1964) Study for book cover illustration
20 x 30 cm
Panther Children's Books
Jethro Arnold Dalton R.A. (1916–1976)

Pryderi wandered the ancient woodland, dressed in the skins of animals, carrying his arrow and bow, with no idea of who he really was or what destiny awaited him. The forest had been his home for as long as he could remember; the beasts living there his only friends and companions. He knew them all by name: the birds that nested in the trees above his head; the squirrels that lived in the branches; the badgers, foxes and rabbits who made their homes among the roots; the boars rooting in the undergrowth; the deer wandering through the glades. He lived in this way, knowing nothing of humankind, until one day . . .

'Until one day, what?' Richard turned to look up at Clio. He had been leaning against her, listening to the story she was telling him, lulled by her voice, half drowsing in the warmth of the sun. Then suddenly she had broken off. 'What happens next?'

'I don't know.' She shrugged. 'We have to make it up. That's the fun of stories.'

Richard sat up, slightly annoyed. He felt cheated by such abrupt emptiness. He wanted the story to be complete. He wanted her to go on.

'OK, OK.' She grinned at the sulky look on his face and pulled him back to rest his head on her lap. 'Pryderi had by now grown exceedingly fair, with blue eyes and bright golden locks.' She laughed, running her fingers through his hair. 'But he had no way of knowing how beautiful he was, because he lived alone in the forest. Until one day . . .'

'Until one day . . .' Richard repeated after her. 'You are playing for time.' He twisted his head to look up at her again. 'You don't know what happens next.'

'Of course I do.' She smiled down at him. 'Until one day he heard the sound of a great horn being blown. Now, he had heard the call of hunting horns before and took care to keep out of the way, for sometimes Arawn Silver-Tongue, great King of the Other World, hunted here with his mighty hounds. Terrible beasts they were, with snow-white fur and glistening red ears, almost as terrifying as their master. Arawn's horn and the yelling of his hounds struck fear into any mortal who heard them, but the sound of this horn was far sweeter, and seemed to draw him on, until he was running through the glades, vaulting fallen boughs, leaping over swift-running streams trying to answer its summons.

'At length he came to a clearing, right in the heart of the wood. At the centre was a knight, seated astride a grey dappled steed. He took the great curving horn from his lips, and turned his helmeted head to Pryderi.

'"What took you so long?"

'Before the youth could reply, the knight slid down from his saddle and came towards him.

'"I am here at the request of my father, the King," the knight announced, removing his helm and shaking out his long dark hair.

'Pryderi realized that this was no knight, but a woman armoured in white metal and gold. She was the most beautiful maiden in the world . . .'

'How did he know she was a maiden?'

'Of course she was!' Clio looked shocked. 'All girls were maidens back then.'

'OK, how did he know she was the most beautiful one if he'd never seen any girls before?'

'He just did, that's all. He didn't need to have seen any others to know that. Anyway, shh! Hush!' She cuffed him lightly across the head. 'Stop interrupting the story. Now, where was I? Ah, yes . . .

'Pryderi was instantly under her spell and knew that he would go to the ends of the earth, do anything for her.

'"My father has sent out knights, far and wide, searching in all parts of the realm for a youth, both fair of face and pure in heart, and I believe that I have found him. Come." She beckoned for him to join her. "The King has declared that a great quest will take place to find the Sangraal, the Holy Grail, the most sacred relic in the whole of

Christendom, and that you shall be part of it. Do you consent?"'

'The youth nodded and knelt before her without her bidding. She drew her sword and touched the blade to one shoulder, then the other.

'"Arise, Sir Knight," she said. "You are now a member of the King's High Court. We will journey on together . . ."

'So began *The Chronicles of Pryderi*.'

'What happens next?' Richard turned his face up to hers.

'That's up to us,' she murmured, touching his cheek. 'Do you agree to undertake the quest?'

Richard nodded, desire for her closing his throat, leaving him unable to speak.

'Very well.' She leaned down to kiss him, her long hair, warm from the sun, cloaking them both.

So began *The Chronicles of Pryderi*. Richard was Pryderi, Grail Knight. Clio was the daughter of the High King, in disguise as a knight with no device. They met in the golden afternoon as the day began to turn towards evening and spent their time together searching for the Sangraal. As darkness fell they went back to their bower high above the hidden valley, where they had other games to play.

The 'quest' took them all over the forest, whooping and calling, shouting and laughing, living inside an increasingly elaborate fantasy of her telling, acting out an epic adventure of their own making.

Clio had never played like this before and she took a deep delight in it. She had been to lots of places and had lived in a series of different communities, but she seemed to have spent most of her time with adults.

Richard was fascinated by the life she'd led, so different from his own, from anything he'd ever known. She'd lived in Morocco and Italy, but it was quite difficult to get her to talk about it.

'What was it like?' he asked her.

'Oh, you know . . .' she said, when he obviously didn't. 'Quite boring, actually.' Richard frowned. How could it be? 'Let's talk about you instead.'

'No.' He shook his head. 'My life's boring. I want to know where you lived. What you did.'

'We spent a lot of time abroad, travelling around. First in Italy – but I was too young to remember much about that – then in Morocco.'

Richard pressed her for more, but all the memories she was prepared to share with him made her experiences seem as boring and mundane as his own. He began to think she was doing it on purpose to punish him for asking in the first place. She described endless afternoons spent in anonymous apartments, drinking sickly cordials, or sweet mint tea, thumbing through a few falling-apart, dog-eared paperbacks that she'd read a hundred times before while flies made geometric patterns under a circling ceiling fan.

'Jay was hardly ever there, always out meeting friends, or off somewhere on some painting expedition. Joe was at school in England. I was left with Lucia.'

'What was it like, though? The people, the country.' Richard had never been abroad. For holidays they had the caravan and his parents considered the foreign trips his school offered to be far too dear.

'It was always too hot to do anything, and I didn't like going out anyway. Men followed us everywhere because Lucia refused to cover up anything, let alone her hair. And there was this beggar right by our building. He had a pink, soft hole where his nose should have been, and his mouth was all twisted about. I knew that I ought to feel sorry for him, or it could have been a her – it was hard to tell under the rags – but I just felt disgusted. Nauseous. It made a kind of mewling, snuffling sound – asking for money, I suppose. And as soon as it saw anyone, it would scuffle forward on legs that were knotted like twigs. I didn't know if that was why the creature begged, or if sitting begging all day had made it grow that way. Lucia nearly always gave something, but still the hands pushed up at us. The fingers were all plaited together.' She shuddered. 'They looked like a squashed leather cup.'

'Yes, but . . .' Richard was still wondering what mint tea tasted like.

'But nothing. How many times do I have to tell you? It was boring! I always seemed to be waiting for Lucia to finish with one of her lovers – ageing French counts, or they said they were. Lucia's a sucker for a title. Blokes in crumpled white suits. Moroccans in jeans and bomber jackets. They were always young. And good-looking. She had them for fun.'

'Didn't Jay care?' Richard asked her.

'No, he . . .' She was about to say something and checked herself. 'It doesn't matter how many she has. It's not what he cares about.'

In the end, Clio had begged to be sent to school in England, like Joe.

'That was even worse. I thought it would be like the boarding school books I'd read, but it wasn't at all. I thought I'd be popular, solve mysteries, have loads of friends – or at least a couple of trusted ones – but all the girls thought I was weird because I didn't have ponies and my parents didn't live in the Home Counties. And if they actually turned up for anything . . .' Clio shuddered at the memory. 'It's OK now, though.'

'Why's that?'

'I go to a different school.' She tapped the jewel that she wore in the side of her nose. 'All the girls there think I'm cool.' She took a drag on a joint she'd brought with her. 'You want some of this?'

Richard shook his head. That was as much as he was likely to get out of her. She wanted to get back to the game. He was happy enough to comply. It seemed that he was living in a much younger time, rediscovering lost childhood delights: coconut candy, liquorice allsorts, but these were delights spiked with a distinct and different flavour. The favours given and boons granted tended to be of a very adult kind. They made love everywhere: in ancient groves, leaf-filled hollows, hidden meadows.

They played the game for days and nights, all the time they were together, expanding the limits of their quest, exploring further and further, until they came to the most magical place of all.

'The Chapel Perilous', from
The Chronicles of Pryderi

(1964) Illustration: pen and ink

17.8 x 12.7 cm

Panther Children's Books

Jethro Arnold Dalton R.A. (1916–1976)

'Behold! The Chapel Perilous!' The knight pointed to the clearing. 'Take care how you approach. Take care lest misadventure should stain your heart and lead to woe . . .'

(Caption below the illustration)

She issued her warning and stood back. Richard could hardly believe what he saw in front of him. Within a circle of ancient trees, surrounded by a meadow, there was a ruined chapel . . .

This was their goal, the place where the Grail resided. And it was so perfect. It was as if she had conjured up a vision out of nothing, but it was real. A real place. She must have known it was here, but even so. He almost believed that if he was to enter, then he would find the fabled Grail. He went forward, pushing back the gnarled lichen-laden branches to take a closer look. The church was tiny, a low grey stone building. A stumpy tower stood at one end of the roofless chancel where the walls reached just above the narrow lancet windows. A large yew tree shadowed the low arched doorway and ivy grasped one side of the building, writhing around the windows like living tracery.

The chapel stood at the centre of a meadow. Richard stepped out into the sunlight, pushing his way through waist-high grass, trailing his hands through silky tops, pale as flax, bent with the weight of seed. The field was studded with flowers. Butterflies rose from the red and blue of poppies and cornflowers and fragrant creamy meadowsweet. Beyond a further brake of trees lay the sea.

'One moment, Sir Knight.' He felt her hand on his shoulder; her voice a low urgent whisper; her breath warm on his neck. 'Before you meet your destiny, I crave one more boon of you . . .'

He laughed as she pulled him into the grass.

'Mâth the Magician', from
The Chronicles of Pryderi

(1964) Illustration: pen and ink
(not used in the published edition)
17.8 x 12.7 cm
Panther Children's Books
Jethro Arnold Dalton R.A. (1916–1976)

Q: You famously never paint yourself, not in recent years, anyway, but this is obviously a bit of a self-portrait. Why is that?
A: Mâth Ap Mathonwy is the primary Druid in the British tradition. Druids were distinct from the others in the tribe because of their gifts. They were known as the people of art. The gifted ones. I like that. I find a lot of similarity between magician and artist. Mâth was a transformer. A shape-shifter. I like to think that's what I do: take a subject and transform it into something else altogether. That's not what I like most about Mâth, though. I like the legend where he gets together with Gwydion, another magician, and they make a woman from flowers, Blodeuwedd. But they cock it up. They can't control their creation. She betrays them and eventually has to be turned into an owl. A magician who occasionally gets it wrong – [laughs] that's good.

(*Arts in Context*, June 1974. Interviewer: Charles Hammond.)

It was some time before Richard could resume the last part of his quest. He stood up from the bower that they had made together, combing grass seeds out of his hair. The door was still some distance away, but as he approached he detected shadowy movement. There was somebody inside the chapel.

It was as if the story they had been spinning had taken on a life of its own. There was a man hunched over where the altar would have stood. It was as if they had surprised Mâth the Magician conjuring spells. He wore a long black gown, and his hair hung down like silver and ebony snakes twisted together.

He turned, tall and stern, thin lips set pale inside a white-streaked beard. Thick curling eyebrows met over his fleshy hooked nose. His skin was burned deep brown; his tilted eyes were as black as sloes. He looked as if he came from somewhere far and distant: Outer Mongolia, or Siberia. A place where they still had shamans. A place very far from here. He stared as they approached, looking from Richard to the girl and back again, his eyes deep beyond fathoming. Richard felt his nervousness flicker into fear.

'What are you doing here?' Clio spoke first.

'I could ask you the same thing,' the artist replied, and smiled.

There was something about the way he looked at them, his grin, that made Richard wonder if this was not a set-up. A deliberately engineered meeting. Or was the man here accidentally? Richard could not make up his mind, and had no way of knowing, but he felt a vague unease, a feeling that everything was not as it appeared to be. Something unspoken was definitely passing between the man and the girl.

'I've been for a swim.' The artist shook his hair out, spreading it across his shoulders. 'I came up here to do some backgrounds for a painting. Come and have a look.'

He went back to where he had been working: a portable folding table was set out with sketchbook and palette. Richard hung back, unsure what to do, how to behave. Had he seen them in the long grass? The chair had its back to the entrance and the open page of his book showed patches of grey stone and curving, curling ivy. The paint was wet, as if he really had been working on that. Even so, he still might have seen them. The soft smile on the man's mouth made him think that maybe he had. To be seen. Caught in the act, Richard felt ready to bolt. Running off might look odd, but Richard really didn't care. The embarrassment, the humiliation would be more than he could bear. If he saw any of them ever again, it would be too soon.

'Aren't you the lad who came to the house the other day?' the artist asked. 'Didn't Lucia call you Ricardo?'

'Yes,' Richard replied. 'That's me. Richard, actually,' he added.

The artist smiled. 'I sent Clio to find you. Didn't she say?'

'No.' Richard looked at Clio, who looked away.

'I want to paint you.'

'Me?' Richard was astonished. 'Why?'

'I don't always choose my subjects, sometimes they choose me.' The artist shrugged. The brush clicked against the glass of the jar. 'Lucia thinks I should, too. She's good at deciding such things. That's why I call her my muse.' He threw away the dirty water and began to pack his things into a battered old leather bag. 'Why don't you come back with us? You can give me a hand carrying this stuff.' He put his hand on the back of the chair. 'Stay for supper. You'd like that, wouldn't you, Clio?'

He looked over to the girl, who didn't reply. Neither did she help Richard with the folding table and chair. She just stood picking ivy off the crumbling wall. Richard tucked the furniture under his arm. The things were quite heavy and awkward to carry, and he didn't know how he'd make conversation with this man all the way back now that Clio seemed to have given up talking altogether. Maybe she'd been struck by one of her intuitions again. It certainly didn't look like she was going to offer to carry anything. Despite his misgivings, Richard felt obliged to give the man a hand.

'I hear you've been spending time up at the Druids' Grove,' he said as they walked.

Richard looked blank.

'The copse at the top of the valley. There's a hidden cave under the overhang.'

'Oh, yes. Yes, we have.' Richard glanced over at Clio. Did she tell them everything? 'I didn't know it was called that.'

The man nodded. 'I used to spend time up there when I was a lad. With my brother. His name was Richard.' He looked down at the boy walking by his side, then looked away. 'You even have a look of him. Coincidence, eh? Lucia would no doubt call it a synchronicity.'

'It's a common enough name,' Richard replied.

'Then maybe, not so much now. We came here every summer. Used to camp out up there. Had stuff stored in an old tin trunk.'

'Really?' Richard's face lit up. 'Me and Dylan – Dylan,

77

he's my friend, you know him, lives at the farm? We found it! We always wondered who it belonged to!'

'Ah, well.' The man smiled. 'There you are! We had some good times playing in the woods up there, me and my brother . . .' He rested a hand on Richard's shoulder, his eyes suddenly cloudy with memory, as opaque as flints. 'Sometimes we wouldn't come home for days. I'm glad you put our things to good use.'

When Richard first saw him, he'd thought the artist quite formidable, that he would be unapproachable, but here they were chatting on about the woods and the games they'd played as if there was almost no difference between them. Questions and answers flowed from one to the other, relaxed and natural. Richard walked by his side, enjoying their conversation. The folding table and chair no longer felt heavy to him and before he knew it, they were at the Wish House.

They had been walking down a narrow rutted lane that didn't see much traffic. Grass grew down the centre. Brambles, wild roses and hazel sprang out from high banks narrowing it further, arching overhead until it seemed as if they were passing down a green tunnel. Suddenly, there it was. They had arrived at the front of the house.

From this aspect, the place looked totally different. Much grander in some ways, but more decayed. Rusting wrought-iron gates were pushed permanently back from two tall stone pillars. Weeds and moss grew in the gravel of the circular drive and a broken asphalt path led to an imposing porch, but the front entrance was never used. Paint peeled from the pillars and balustrades. The heavy wooden door had swollen, making it almost impossible to open. The whole area was shaded, partly by the house, but also by foliage crowding in from either side. Tall trees grew up the banks which flanked the house. The garden was bordered by thick hedges of yew, hawthorn and laurel which had grown for years without any blade touching them and were now the size of young trees. Richard thought of the square-cut privet around his own suburban garden, how his dad was forever going out to shave the lawn and give the hedges a short back and sides.

On one side of the drive, leggy roses struggled through the long dry grass. The other side must have been an orchard at one time; a few gnarled old apple trees survived, crusted with curling patches of green-grey lichen. The central island had been planted in a pattern of little flower beds surrounded with low hedges. Richard recognized the dull tired-looking foliage and the sharp dog-fox smell of box. This was the garden he'd glimpsed from the window the first day he was here. He'd seen knot gardens like this before, in the gardens of country houses on family visits, and when he went to Stratford-on-Avon with the school. This one was different. He paused to survey it. The beds were set out in triangles and most of the flowers that grew in them were black.

The Witches' Garden

(1978) Multimedia collage construction
115.3 x 86 cm
Clio Dalton (1960–)
Art School First-Year Show

A knot garden through a central window. Low box hedges surround unusual plants: tall puce foxgloves, deep purple monkshood, pale rue, yellow wormwood, dark green belladonna.

On one side of the window, curling pages torn from different herbals pinned to a cork notice board bring the plants into the domestic environment and offer other perspectives on the plants growing outside. Foxglove, hemlock, henbane, monkshood, belladonna are shown in meticulous botanical detail. Deadly but beautiful, poisonous but with healing properties, they set up a duality repeated by the objects ranged along shelves: unlabelled pots of purple fruit; scarlet toadstools mixed in a basket of mushrooms; small blue and green bottles of ribbed glass. By emphasizing the unwholesomeness that lies beneath the wholesome, this unsettling piece reminds us that there is no such thing as innocence. Nothing is as it seems, the artist appears to be telling us. Nothing can be trusted.

(Notes accompanying)

Jay disappeared round the side of the house, with a 'See you later,' and a nonchalant wave.

Richard stared at the herb bed.

'That is bizarre.'

'That's because it's a Witches' Garden,' Clio explained. 'It's set out in a pentacle.' These were the first words she'd spoken to him since they'd left the ruined chapel. 'A five-pointed star with a five-sided figure in the middle. It's a kind of joke because it's like a herb garden but not. A fair few of the plants are poisonous and some of them are black.' She pointed to the drooping monkshood, the pendulous night-shade with its shiny dark berries. 'That's henbane.' The plant had bell-shaped flowers with petals the colour of dried skin, lined with dark veins and paper-thin. 'Witches used it to make flying ointment. It's quite rare now, apparently. And that's a castor oil plant.' She pointed to a shrub with bright green leathery leaves shaped like out-spread hands. 'See these?' She picked a prickly red seed capsule, splitting the casing to show three shiny, mottled beans. 'They produce ricin, one of the deadliest poisons known to man.'

Richard took a step backwards. He hoped she was going to wash her hands.

'It's not *The Day of the Triffids*!' Clio laughed. 'They aren't going to jump up and bite you. They're just plants.'

'I know that!' Richard stepped forward again, feeling slightly foolish.

They were as innocent as any other flowers, of course.

Nevertheless, there was a corrupted beauty about them, a fascination. The power to kill lay within the variegated greenery, the hairy leaves, purple blotched stems, pendulous berries and drooping heads. They attracted flies rather than bees or butterflies. The strength of the sun drew a pungent, slightly musky scent from them, just this side of unpleasant. A warning to the unwary.

'Is Lucia really a witch, then?' Richard asked Clio.

'Of course I am.'

Richard turned around, startled. He looked about, scanning the upstairs windows, examining the tangled hedges, trying to locate the disembodied voice. He discovered her by her laughter. She was at the open window of the little larder, leaning on the sill.

'Nothing hidden. Nothing forbidden. Blessed be the goddess. Do what though wilt shall be the whole law.'

She recited the words in a mocking, ironic chant. Clio joined in from the other side of him. Their voices were very similar. The effect was stereophonic. Richard looked from one to the other, caught in the web of words and laughter, not entirely sure that they were joking. He laughed, too, an unconvincing whinny that failed to hide how disconcerted he felt.

'It's nice to see you again, Richard,' Lucia gave him a wide warm smile. 'I said not to be a stranger. It's very selfish of you, Clio, to keep him all to yourself. And what are they doing? Making you lug furniture about? Leave it in the porch. We've got people here. You must come and join us. Clio,' she addressed her daughter, 'I need you to help.'

Lucia withdrew from the window, disappearing into the house. Voices rose in greeting as she rejoined her guests. Glass clinked on glass. The acrid whiff of marijuana drifted on the air. There was music coming from Joe's sound system. Not Moroccan this time. 'Tubular Bells'. It sounded like quite a party.

'Who's there?' Richard asked Clio. He glanced to where the drive curved down to the garage and outhouses. There were cars parked down there. Dalton's Citroën had been joined by an old Jag, a VW camper van, a Deux Cheveux and a Renault 4.

She shrugged. 'Meg and the rest of the family. They're here for the weekend. Come on.'

She looked impatient to join them, as if it wasn't enough just to be with him any more.

'Who's Meg?' Richard asked.

'Jay's first wife,' she explained again. 'I told you. She'll be with Naeve and Freya, my half-sisters. You'll like them—'

'How many have you got?' he interrupted, although he remembered now. How did she know if he would like them or not? She was talking to him as though he was a halfwit, and that annoyed him.

'Two, and a half-brother. He won't be here. He's in Afghanistan or somewhere. They're all much older than me. Naeve and Freya will have brought people with them, and then there's the children. I'm an aunt. I've got loads of nephews and nieces.' She laughed. 'Some of them are older than me.'

'Hey, hang on! You didn't tell me you had a whole other family!'

'Didn't I? Well, never mind.' She grabbed his hand. 'Come along and meet them. They're fun.'

'No, thanks.' Richard shook his head. He didn't want to meet a whole new set of people. He found it hard enough with the members of the family he'd met already. 'I'd better be getting back.'

'Why?'

'I just have to, that's all. You know. Parents.' Clio looked as though she didn't. 'They'll be missing me.'

'I thought they didn't care where you went. What you did.'

'There are limits.'

He didn't want to explain why he had to go. He didn't really know why himself. He could just imagine them, people from London, stretched out on the lawn, lounging about, smoking and drinking, laughing in ways that would make him uncomfortable, talking about things he probably wouldn't understand. Suddenly, he wanted to be surrounded by the mundane and ordinary: toilet blocks and lines of washing. He wanted to go back to the caravan site. Besides, they *might* be missing him. Maybe they *were* worrying. He felt a tiny stab of guilt. It was time to get back.

'Don't you want to stay with me?' She smiled at him, her eyes half shut. 'You can stay the night. Lucia won't mind . . .'

'Can't,' he said, shaking his head again. 'Can't stay out two nights in a row. Anyway, it would be different. Different from when there's just you and me.'

'But Jay will be expecting you.' The corners of her mouth turned down, petulant.

'So what? He'll see me again, won't he?'

'Maybe,' she said, turning away from him. 'Maybe not.'

She walked away, arms folded, without a backward glance.

Richard was left staring at the Witches' Garden without really seeing it. He immediately regretted his stubbornness. He was a coward, he told himself. Afraid of meeting these other people because he wasn't like them. They might laugh at him, his clothes, the way he spoke, his ordinariness. He just wanted to be with her and didn't want to share her or feel himself subside, diminish in her eyes.

Something could break between them if he did not follow, but every second he stayed made going after her that much more difficult.

'She's lost him for you,' Lucia remarked to her husband when Clio joined the party alone.

'He'll come back.' Jay smiled at his wife, winding a strand of her vibrant hair in between his dark fingers. 'Like mother, like daughter. They always do for you.'

Lucia returned his smile. 'How did you know where she'd find him?'

The artist tapped his nose and winked at her. 'I'm a magician. Didn't you know?'

Lucia laughed her deep-throated chuckle. 'No, I mean really!'

'Boys are like dogs.' The artist sighed. 'They always visit the same places, as though they have to put down their scent. He came here, where he'd been before with that boy from the farm.'

'Dylan?'

'That's him. I saw them last year, when I came back to look the place over. I took a walk up to Druids' Grove and found it already occupied. So I thought he might go up there.'

'Clever. So you sent Clio up there to find him?'

'I didn't know for sure that she would.' Jay shrugged, twitching the hem of his voluminous djellaba. 'But I thought it a distinct possibility.'

'Things seem to have gone beyond just *finding* him. She's hardly been home since.'

'Boy like that? Girl like her? It's all about harnessing the forces of nature. That's what we magicians do.'

'Why all the mystery? I don't understand why you didn't just ask him to pose for you.'

'Why the mystery?' Jay arched an eyebrow. 'I thought you thrived on it. The painting is not the only thing I want from him.'

'What else could there be?'

Jay surveyed the gathering guests. 'Sometimes I need a change of people. Who else is coming?'

'Hammond, and he's bringing Martin.'

Jay grimaced. Martin was the son of Naeve's ex-partner, which made him some kind of grandson. Jay hadn't liked the father, and he didn't like the boy much either. He liked Hammond even less.

'What does Hammond want?'

'You *know* what he wants.'

'Well, when he does come, you can tell him I'm not selling.' Jay stood up. 'I'm going down to the beach.'

Page b/w contact prints of Clio

Dear Clio,

Thought you might like to have a look at these.
Some of them ain't half bad - he said modestly
- considering the material I had to work with!!!
No - seriously - let me know if you want me to
work any of them up. Don't forget the portfolio
- I know a guy who knows a guy!

Love 'n' kisses,

Martin xxx

(Note written on the back)

Richard left the Wish House, following the high-sided lane down towards the village. Farm gates gave off to the left and right and he had to watch his footing; the incline was steep and fresh cowpats mired the ground. To slip and get covered in shit, that was all he needed, but he was glad that he'd left now. Things were getting too much, too heavy. He wanted a break from her. He looked out for Dylan as he neared the farm, but there was no sign of him in the yard. A sheepdog ran out; his furious staccato barking startled Richard. The dog was young, with a patch of tan fur on one leg like a sock. He stopped barking and started growling instead, keeping a wary distance. Richard thought of swaggering up like Dylan would, calling his bluff, ordering him back into the yard. Instead, he crossed over and passed on the opposite side of the lane.

There were other things to do, he thought, as he went on his way. He could find Dylan later. Go down to the pub tonight, see if he was there. Then maybe they could do something. Go to Carmarthen. Or Tenby. Bound to be something going on. There were pubs he could probably get into if he wore jeans and a sweater. There could be a fair, or a disco. They might even meet some girls. He didn't have to go back to the Wish House. Maybe he wouldn't go back at all. He wasn't dependent, that was for sure.

Richard did not go out. He stayed in the caravan. The next day, he found himself walking up the lane again. The lane that led to the Wish House. Jay. Clio. Lucia. Clio. Lucia.

Jay. The names chimed with his stride. He couldn't stop thinking about them. They occupied his mind. Sometimes all at the same time. He rounded a corner, to find his way blocked by a tractor. The driver leaned down, cutting the engine.

'Hey, Rick, man,' Dylan shouted. 'Good to see you. What you been up to?'

Richard stuck his hands in his pockets and shrugged. 'Nothing much.'

Dylan swung himself down.

'What you doing? Going up to the hippie place?'

'Yeah,' he announced, wanting it to come out slowly, 'as a matter of fact. I met the girl again . . .'

'Clio?'

Richard blushed in spite of himself.

'She was down the pub last night with her brother and this bloke called Martin, who was even thinner. Looked like a skinhead but talked posh. They were with some others. Wild night. You should have been there.' Dylan paused, penny dropping. 'You have been though, haven't you? You dirty little devil!'

Richard grinned and put on a bit of a swagger.

'Might have.'

'You'll be all right there, mate.' Dylan grinned and winked. 'She knows all the moves, like.'

'Yeah?' Richard waited a second before asking. 'What do you mean, exactly?'

'She's a right bike.'

'How do you know?'

'How do you think?' He gave a wink and glanced over at Richard, who was staring at the ground now trying to get a hold of himself.

'So you . . .'

'Course that!' Dylan laughed. 'Me and half the blokes in the village.'

'You didn't tell me!'

'You didn't ask! Told you they were into all that.' He held up two fingers. 'Love and peace, man. Don't tell me you thought you were her one and only? That it was true love! Christ, Rick. Get a grip, will you?' Dylan threw his arm round him. 'You busted your cherry – that's what matters – and you couldn't have chosen better for getting started. She's a real goer.'

Richard wanted to shrug off the consoling arm, wanted to punch Dylan's grinning face until the hot shiny eyes blurred with tears, but to do so would be to show how much he cared, how what Dylan said had hurt him. It didn't occur to him to doubt Dylan's word. What reason did Dylan have to lie to him? She was so good at it, guiding his fumbling, so sure of her own enjoyment, ferocious in the pursuit of her own pleasure. In his heart, Richard knew it was all true. He'd thought it himself.

'This needs celebrating!' Dylan hugged him tighter, trying to cheer him up. 'What say we get hold of a couple of flagons and go down the beach tonight? Build a fire. Get pissed. Like old times. I've hardly seen you this summer.'

'Yeah,' Richard muttered. 'Could do, I suppose.'

'Great! I'll meet you down there. Half seven all right?'

'OK.' Richard felt his mood lift, just a little bit. A cookout on the beach, along with a few illicit drinks. That was how it used to be.

'It'll be great, man. I'll get the cider. You scrounge up some grub – sausages and that.' He climbed back into the cab.

'Wait on! Where are you going?'

Richard put a foot on the running board. He didn't want

Dylan to leave him. He certainly wasn't going up to the Wish House now.

'Collecting bales from the upper field,' Dylan looked down at the younger boy. 'I could do with a hand. Want to come?'

'Yeah. Why not?'

'Hop in the trailer, then. Let's go!'

Dylan started the engine and Richard jumped on the back with Jesse the sheepdog. It was work with Dylan, or spend another day at a loose end. Anyway, it might be fun.

They finished about five and Richard went to the shower block. Most people hadn't come back from the beach yet, so there was plenty of hot water. He stood letting it play over him, soothing the pain from his burned shoulders and aching back. His hands had blisters all across the palms, it hurt to hold the soap, but he'd had a brilliant day. It had been a great laugh and he had managed to keep up with Dylan pretty well. He was proud of himself.

Dylan came by about seven o'clock and they made their way through the Burrows, the local name for the area of tough grass and dune that came immediately before the beach. Richard stopped on the last of the duckboards as the whole wide expanse opened up before him. There were still some people about: kids running around, a few hardy bathers still in the water, although the beach was not ideal for swimming. Even at high tide the water was shallow, barely reaching the thighs. At low tide it practically disappeared altogether, leaving a gleaming expense of sand and treacherous mud. The water, if you ever got to it, was subject to rip tides and vicious river currents. No one in their right mind would swim there then. Couples walked their dogs on the long golden curve of the beach. He took a minute, fitting the actual scene to his memory of it. He didn't care much about the swimming; he loved this place. He dreamed about it, probably would all his life.

He adjusted his rucksack on his sore, sunburned shoulders and started off with Dylan. They walked towards a jutting outcrop of rock which lay like a fold in the beach, a long crease that marked the limit of the most populated areas. The dunes gave way to cliffs here and ribs of smooth, purple grey rock that curved down towards the sea, fissured and split with long gaping cracks that the receding tide made into pools. Richard and Dylan jumped over these and splashed through the shallow rippling streams that ran from the cliffs and disappeared into the sands. They wandered along collecting driftwood until they had enough to get a fire going. Then they searched for and found the good place, the place they always went: a cleft in the cliff that gave extra shelter.

The sun was falling into the west as Dylan built a hearth from boulders and slabs of rock and began the careful construction of the fire. He'd brought some spuds and he put them in the bottom to roast, packing the twigs and branches round them. Richard went off to find more wood. The sun was going now, sinking behind a distant headland, adding ripples of gold to the ribbons of red and purple cloud streaming out over the sea. The beach fell into shadow and Richard could see that there was another party going on further down from them. The beach made distances deceptive, but it had to be the people from the Wish House. There was a little jetty, and that part of the beach was directly below the house. The sound of voices talking and laughing carried over the flat expanse of sand. The beach could play tricks with sound as well as sight. Suddenly, they seemed very near, as if it should be possible to hear what they were saying, although the words on the wind were just meaningless noise.

The nerve *of these people!*

He could imagine his mother and father talking.

Act like they own everything.

They would work themselves up into a right state.

Why can't they pipe down?

Do they have *to impose themselves like this on the rest of us?*

As he watched, someone streaked down to the sea, chased by someone else. They crashed into the water with screams and shrieks. Even from this distance he could see that they were both naked.

The nerve of these people.

They had a bonfire going. A big one. Sparks flew and scattered as someone threw on more wood. Their little fire would be pathetic in comparison to that. Flames shot up and were taken by the gusting wind, flaring in his direction like a beacon signalling from a different world.

There were two men walking along the foreshore, coming towards him. One of them was Jay, he could tell by the flowing robe. The other was slightly shorter, with dark hair to his shoulders and a Che Guevara moustache. He wore a crumpled linen suit but was barefoot, like Jay, his pale trousers rolled to the knees. The two men were deep in conversation and probably wouldn't even notice him, but Richard turned away. He didn't want it to seem like he was spying. He went off down the beach, pulling his load of wood behind him. Most of it was probably too wet to burn.

'I could be there. If I wanted to,' he told himself, but still he felt excluded. Soon the other party was hidden by a turn in the cliff. He felt relieved, as if he had escaped some invisible scrutiny. Unlikely as that would be. He decided not to tell Dylan about them.

The moon rose, as searingly white as phosphorous, but casting a cold light over everything. Sausages sizzled on a makeshift wire grill, falling in the fire so they had to be rescued with sticks. They talked as they tended the food, but things had changed between them. They both felt it. Dylan was nearly two years older, and now he'd left school and started work he made Richard feel even younger. All his talk was of the farm and working with his father. Dylan was a smart lad; he could have gone on to do A levels, and gone to university. That's what Richard planned to do: he had not considered any alternatives, that was what you did, he'd never thought any further. Dylan had different plans.

'I got the idea from her at the Wish House,' he was saying. 'Gets her eggs from us, see?'

'So?'

Dylan shook his head at the other boy's stupidity.

'She don't like *battery*! She was telling Ma about it. Have to be from farmyard chickens. Meat, too. Beef and lamb from animals grazing naturally. I told Dad. It's not just her. There's more like them, and they'll pay more for quality. And veg. Grown without chemical fertilizers and pesticides and that. Gramps used to go on about it. Not natural, he said. Affects the taste and everything. Dad can't see it, but I reckon there's money in it. He's going to let me have a go at any rate.'

He was full of schemes for the future.

'Take the caravan site – Dad wanted to sell it off.'

'Oh?' That was news to Richard.

'Yeah, he was talking about it last year. But I've persuaded him to invest in it. Expand it ourselves. Have more permanent units. Maybe build some cabins, or convert

97

some of the farm outbuildings into holiday homes. Use money from that to reinvest and expand the specialist side of the farm business. You got to diversify see, Rick – can't stay at the same place forever. You got to move on.'

While he talked, he drew little squares in the sand with a stick to show different areas of the business and how they would link together. It was like listening to a full-grown man. In a way, Richard envied him. He knew exactly what he wanted to do, and he was doing it, while Richard himself still didn't have any idea.

'Do you reckon the spuds are done?' he asked, to break up the monologue. He could only take so much detail about relative yields, however much he might admire Dylan's enterprise and knowledge.

'Dunno.' Dylan poked at the fire. 'Sausages are, though. Let's have a look.'

The sausages were half-cindered, but they ate them anyway, washed down with draughts of sweet-tasting cider. Then they raked the spuds out, cracking open the blackened skins, scooping out the creamy insides with shells. They munched and chewed in silence. Before, Richard would not have noticed the black burned bits, the potatoes' gritty ashiness, the constant feel of sand in the mouth. Such things had added savour to the feast, but now he felt like gagging. It was just not the same somehow.

The embers were rapidly cooling, their cherry-red glare giving way to the darkness all around. They had eaten everything and finished the cider. Time to go home. Dylan felt the same and they were just about to get up and kick sand over what was left of the fire when a figure came up out of the darkness. It was Clio. Her wide jeans were cut low on the hip and her cropped sweater was riding up to show her flat brown stomach. She was not wearing a bra.

The ribbed wool stretched tight over her breasts, showing her nipples. Neither of the boys said a word.

'Hello!' She smiled at them. 'Fancy seeing you here!'

'Yeah,' Richard said, finally. 'Fancy. Must be Lucia's synchronicity.'

'I told you it worked!' Her smile widened. 'I was just wandering along, looking for more wood, when I saw your fire. Great night for the beach, isn't it?' She glanced down at their ashy remnants, the empty flagons of cider. 'We've got quite a party going. Plenty left. Why don't you join us?'

She was speaking to both of them, but looking at Richard. She turned, expecting them to follow. The two boys stared at each other.

'Synchriwhat?' Dylan raised his eyebrows, his mouth quirking at the corners as he tried to hold back a spluttering laugh. 'Come on, man.' He nudged Richard with his shoulder. 'She said there was more drink. Let's go!'

Richard shook his head.

'You go,' he muttered, so she wouldn't hear him.

'Don't be daft, man! You got to take what's on offer!'

Dylan grabbed Richard round the shoulders and turned him to follow Clio down the beach.

Even though the bonfire had begun to fall into glowing embers, the whole area was illuminated. Small lanterns hung from driftwood branches and candles flickered inside coloured jars stuck into the sand. A folding table was laden with food and all kinds of different bottles. People sat perched on logs or lounged on multicoloured rugs and blankets. It looked like a fairy feast, or something from a legend: people dressed in bright clothes; the spread banquet, the little lights shining out. Jay sat on an upturned log set like a throne at the centre of the chosen people. He looked like a king, or some god of the sea with his court gathered around him. He was talking, his arms stretched out from the wide sleeves of his loose-fitting gown, his long hair falling forward and the silver in his beard catching the light.

A photographer was climbing over things on spider-thin legs, trampling on people with his heavy fourteen-hole Docs, trying to get as near to Jay as possible. Richard felt a tug of jealousy. That must be the guy Dylan had been talking about, the one who was with Clio in the pub last night. The photographer's flash lit up Jay's face, making him blink and startle. That would be a nice one for the album. He put his hand up to block another shot and carried on talking to the bloke he'd been walking with on the beach. The photographer turned his attention to Clio, who was standing near them. She laughed, posing, and walked off with him following. They looked like they were having fun.

'Ricardo!' Lucia called in a high carrying voice that made everyone turn his way. Everyone except Clio. '*Ciao, bambino, ciao!*'

She kissed him on both cheeks. No one in his family did this. He froze into awkwardness and managed to turn the wrong way, almost kissing her on the mouth and bumping her nose with his. She laughed and said, 'You need more practice!' before turning her attention to Dylan.

'Dylan! Welcome!' She put her arm round the older boy. 'Well done, Clio, at finding you two!' She clutched them both to her. 'Now, you boys must be hungry. I always prepare much too much, so there's plenty left. I've just put more kebabs on, they should be done now. I do so love this: eating outdoors, cooking on an open fire. It reminds me of Morocco when the Tuareg used to gather. Try these.'

She took an embroidered cloth and picked up several skewers, putting them on to a plate. Richard took one gingerly, nibbling at the still sizzling meat. It looked like a sausage on a stick. It was hot, not just burning to his mouth, but with a powerful spiciness that threatened to numb his tongue. He waited for it to cool a little and tried a bit more. His mother did not like spicy food, so they never ate it at home. She wouldn't even try Chinese, let alone Indian, so he'd never eaten anything like this before. The taste was unfamiliar, but intriguing.

'Do you like it?' Lucia asked.

He nodded, his mouth full. He decided that he did.

'Try it with this.' She ladled some dark stew on to his plate.

'What is it?'

'Aubergine.'

He'd never even heard of that. He looked blank.

'Some people call it eggplant. It's a purple . . . fruit? Vegetable?' She put her head on one side, as if finding it difficult to decide. 'It grows like tomatoes, or bell peppers. *Very* hard to get hold of round here. I had to have these sent up from London. Try it. See what you think.'

Richard took a mouthful. The stew was flavoured with tomatoes, and spicy again, but he was getting used to that. There was something else about it. He tried another forkful. A strange, soft, melting texture, a velvety richness he'd never tasted before. It made you want more.

'Do you like it?' He nodded. 'What about you, Dylan?'

'Yeah. It's OK. These aubergines. Where do they grow? Could you grow them here?'

Richard took a couple more kebabs and left Dylan talking to Lucia about exotic vegetables.

He watched Clio as she moved from one group of people to another. Half of him wanted her to notice him, the other half was keeping an eye out so he could avoid her if she came anywhere near. She moved with a floating graceful-ness, like a dancer. The photographer was still buzzing about her, making frames with his fingers, taking photo-graphs from stupid angles, like she was a model, or a film star, or something. And she could be. Richard knew it. Jealousy wrenched at his insides as he watched her speak to this person, or that person. It was as though she were bestowing her beauty upon each of them, old or young, making them feel that they were the only one she cared to speak to in the whole world.

She was different, he told himself, different from other girls. Just as this kebab was different from Sunday lamb and mint sauce. Perhaps he was wrong to judge her in the same way, or judge her at all. He still didn't know what he would say to her, so it was probably best not to speak to her, but he couldn't help looking at her and he knew that he was lost. Her beauty tore at him, taking the hurt deeper inside him. Making it worse. There were kids bombing about everywhere, shrieking and screaming, getting on his nerves. Two of them crashed into him and he nearly dropped one of his kebabs in the sand. He gave them a look that sent them scuttling. They should all be in bed. He'd had enough of these people. He didn't belong here. He wanted to go. Now. Get away while he still could.

'Who are you scowling at?'

He'd lost sight of her, just for a moment, and now here she was, right in front of him. The night was getting chilly. She had a brightly patterned blanket wrapped round her shoulders like a shawl.

'Are you avoiding me?'

'No, I'm just . . .'

'Wandering around on your own looking miserable,' she supplied for him. 'What's the matter, Richard?'

'Nothing, I . . .'

'Is it what I said in the Witches' Garden? I just wanted you to stay. I didn't intend to be mean or anything.'

'You weren't.' Richard shook his head. 'It's not that. It's something else.'

'What?' She looked at him. 'Is it Dylan? Has he said something?'

He glanced up at her. How could she know?

'He said you were at the pub last night. With Joe and . . . and some other bloke.'

'Martin? There were others there besides him.' Clio looked puzzled. 'Anyway, I didn't know I was not allowed to go. It's not just that, is it?'

Richard shook his head.

'What else has he been saying?' She narrowed her eyes at the other boy who was still talking to her mother.

'How do you know he's said anything?'

'Call it intuition. What's he been saying? As if I couldn't guess.'

'You and him, and others too, he said you . . . well, you know.' Richard sighed. He really didn't want to talk about this. He turned away, overcome with awkwardness.

She didn't say anything, not for a while, but Richard could tell that she was angry.

'And you believed him?' Her voice shook as she asked the question. He wouldn't look at her; she moved to stand in front of him. 'Of course you did.' She read the misery on his face. She took his chin between her fingers, pinching hard and forcing him to look up at her. 'Didn't occur to you that he might be lying, did it?'

'Why should it?' He shook himself from her grip. 'Why should he?'

'Because you're younger than him. Because he's jealous.

103

Because he's boasting, wants to talk himself up. I can think of lots of reasons.' Clio folded her arms and turned away. 'I've never been with him. Or any of his little friends. I haven't been with any boys. Apart from you.' She turned back and put her arms round him. 'Don't know where they've been, do I?'

Are you sure? he wanted to ask. Are you really sure? But he didn't want to doubt her. It was her word against Dylan's and he wanted to believe her. Dylan could be lying, like she said, talking up his conquests. Lots of boys did that to make you feel bad. It was a common way to make other boys feel small. Giles did it all the time, recounting lurid tales of *his* Saturday night when he knew you'd been at home with your mum and dad watching Parky on the telly.

She took his hand, leading him away from the party. He didn't argue, or ask to know more. His heart beat fast as he followed her into the dunes. The lights of the gathering disappeared behind them. The voices faded. The rhythm of the rise and fall of the surf on the shore matched itself to the thud of his heart, the beat of the words in his head. *I haven't been with any boys. Apart from you . . .* Her words had reassured him, but words mean what you want them to. Her choice allowed him to dismiss his suspicions. It did not occur to him to question them, although she knew far more than he did. That first time she'd known exactly what to do, while he hadn't had a clue.

They walked in the soft sand, through tufts of grey-green spiky marram grass with only the cold moon to guide them. They found a deep place, sliding down the steep banks, landing in a heap at the bottom. The sand was cool and silky to the touch. Clio spread the rug and beckoned him down beside her. He leaned over her, stroking strands of fine hair away from her face. She was pale in the moonlight, her lips slightly parted. He leaned closer, kissing her lightly, then more deeply and, at that moment, he did not care a whole lot what she'd done, or who she'd done it with. She was with him now.

The Witches' Garden

Detail from: Collage construction (1978) Botanical drawings

Sketchbook (handwritten notes)

15.3 x 8.6 cm

Lucy Ivanoff (later Lucia Dalton) (1940–)

MONKSHOOD

ACONITUM NAPELLUS

Native perennial of SW England and S Wales.
Prefers damp woodland and shady stream banks.
Flowers between May and July. Grows up to 1m
high. Large helmet-shaped flowers - from blue to
deep purple-black. One of the most poisonous of
British plants - small amount can cause death in a
very short time.

DEATH CAP

AMANITA PHALLOIDES

Grows from July to October - deciduous and
mixed woodlands. Smooth cap - brownish to
yellow-green, pale green to whitish yellow - gills
always pure white - stem ends in a soft bulb
surrounded by stocking-like volva. Flesh pure white
- delicious taste, sweetish scent, drying specimens
can smell like rotting flowers, or mature cheese.
Deadly poisonous. Up to 95% of people who eat
these mushrooms die.

HEMLOCK

CONIUM MACULATUM

Tall robust biennial. Grows up to 2m. Easily
recognized by spotted stems and unpleasant
smell. Found throughout the British Isles on damp
ground: swamp, river, stream, canals and by coastal
walls. All parts highly toxic. Given as means of
execution in Ancient Greece. Socrates chose to
take hemlock after being condemned for impiety
and corruption of the young.

Richard was late getting up the next day, and when he arrived at the Wish House there was nobody about. The back door was open, but it didn't feel right to go in uninvited. He wandered round to the front of the house and found a woman he'd never seen before. She was on her knees, reaching over the box hedge into the Witches' Garden. A shallow basket, woven from wide split wood slats, stood on little legs on the grass beside her. The only sound came from the bees and the scrape of her digging trowel.

'Um, excuse me,' he began tentatively, not wanting to startle her.

'Hello, there! Where did you spring from?' She turned round quickly, squinting up at him from under a floppy cloth hat decorated with giant pink daisies. 'I was miles away. You quite made me jump.'

'I'm sorry. I didn't mean to. I was just looking . . .'

'For Clio, I would imagine. You're her friend. I recognize you from last night. I'm Meg.'

'Richard,' he said.

'Nice to meet you, Richard. I'd shake your hand, but mine are all grubby.' She looked down at her dirt-covered hands. They were large, with long, squared-off fingers. Like a man's. 'Can't garden without getting my hands in the soil.'

She was big. When she stood up she was taller than Richard, with a broad, brown face, creased and wrinkled now, but still retaining a striking handsomeness. A mass of strong white hair hung down her back in a thick braided club. Bits had escaped, springing out from under her hat and away from her plait in snaky wisps. She wore a pink top and orange trousers patterned with big splotchy lime green flowers, the knees were patched with dust, specked with bits of twig, grass seed and crumbs of earth.

'Clio's gone down to the farm. We've run out of milk and eggs. Jay's gone to the beach to bathe. I don't know where the others are.' She looked around vaguely as if they might all pop out at any moment. 'We were rather late last night. Probably all still in bed. And it's such a lovely day. I've come out to do a spot of gardening. Lucia's let it all go somewhat. In terrible need of water, what with this summer we're having.' She nodded towards a battered metal watering can. 'Want to help?'

Richard nodded, not feeling he had much choice. He toted water back and forth, filling the can from an outside tap, wondering why they couldn't have a hose like his dad. She handed him a pair of secateurs when he'd finished doing that.

'Here,' she indicated the box hedges. 'Snip away at those. As if you were giving them a haircut. No need to be too fussy. That's it. Do you have a garden at home?'

Richard explained that he did. Although his father was the gardener. His mother didn't bother very much. She just liked sitting in it. The house was her domain.

'Dad keeps it . . .' He was going to say, 'very neat'. He settled for: 'Different from this.'

Meg gave a deep rumbling laugh.

'I'll bet! This is different all right. Although they all need tending. No such thing as a wild garden. Particularly this one. All the plants carefully chosen. They only grow like this because Lucia doesn't look after them.' She pointed to

110

different plants. 'Foxglove you probably know and that's wolfsbane, henbane, butcher's broom, mullein, wormwood, liquorice, opium poppy, peony, black cohosh, and mistletoe.'

She pointed out the balls of vivid green clinging to the upper branches of the old apple trees.

'No wonder Clio called it the Witches' Garden,' he said.

She laughed. 'That was Jay's name for it when Lucia and I first talked about planting. So we set it out in a pentacle, just for a joke, and put in some other things, too. Herbs for a witches' brew.' She pinched a bunch of pale leaves between her fingers, sniffing their powerful, bitter scent. 'These are not culinary herbs, that's for certain. But they have their uses. They certainly do.'

They worked on in silence.

'This house was once called Tp y Wraig Hysbys,' she said after a bit. 'Which roughly translates as the house of the wisewoman, sorceress – the Witch's House.'

'I didn't know that.' He told her Dylan's theory about the trees saying, 'I wish . . ., I wish . . .'

'Maybe.' Meg sat back on her heels. 'Who knows? Names are strange, don't you think? Which do you prefer, Richard?'

'I don't know.'

Her words had started a song off in his mind. A Cream tune: 'Strange Brew'. Now it was there, he couldn't get it out of his head. He started humming, just under his breath.

'How quiet it is.' She looked at him. Their eyes were on a level. 'Have you noticed? First thing I noticed when I came here with Jay. I was young. A student. His father was still alive . . .' She gave a sigh. 'Many years ago now. More than I care to count. I was struck straight away by the peacefulness. I like to think of it as a place of ancient

111

healing. There was a monastery near here, did you know that? The house is built with the stone. This may have been their Physic Garden. Sweet marjoram grows wild, so do feverfew, valerian and chamomile.' She touched the herbs as she spoke so that they gave off a faint scent. 'It might even go back before that – to the Druids. You know that axe head Jay keeps in the house? He and his brother found that. People have been here a very long time. I like the idea of that. Continuity.' She looked round to survey their work. 'There, that's better. At least they won't all get choked to death by couch grass.' She threw a thick, coarse swollen-jointed stalk on the pile of weeds that she'd collected. 'Although that has its uses, too. Most plants do.'

She was talking as though he wasn't there.

'You seem to know a lot about it,' Richard said, more to re-establish his presence than anything else.

'Well, I love plants and I love growing them.' She brushed the feathery fronds in front of her as if stroking fur. 'See this? Fennel. I love the texture of it, the colour, the smell.' She rubbed a stem between her fingers and held out her hand. She closed her eyes and they both breathed the delicate aniseed given off by the bruised leaves. 'You can cook with it, or take it to ease digestion, cleanse the blood, repair the liver.'

'How do you know all these things?' Richard asked. 'How do you know what to use for what?'

'A lifetime's study. I'm a doctor.' She looked at him and laughed. 'Don't look so surprised. I gave up conventional medicine a long time ago. Now I'm an alternative practitioner, specializing in natural remedies.'

Richard's brow creased. He couldn't see why anyone would want to stop being a proper doctor. He could imagine his mother's reaction. 'Mumbo-jumbo' she'd call it;

'stuff and nonsense'. She had more drugs in her medicine cabinet than Boots the chemist.

'Enough for today.' Meg stood up, brushing grass and dirt from her knees. 'Would you like a cup of tea? I think we deserve one.'

Richard followed her into the house. He might as well wait here until Clio came back.

The tea was made from fresh herbs that she set about infusing.

'We have regular tea, if you prefer.'

Richard shook his head. He didn't want P.G. or Typhoo. He wanted to be like them. If that's what they drank, then he would, too. Richard wrinkled his nose at the strong sharp smell, but he was determined to try the olive green liquid she offered him.

'Sage and rosemary.' She laughed at the look on his face. 'Don't worry, it'll not poison you. Here, wait for me to add a spoonful of honey. It's good for the blood.' She blew steam from the top of her hot brew. 'It must be confusing for you, all these new people. We're quite a tribe when we're all together.'

Richard took an experimental sip and wondered if there was any way of disposing of it, other than drinking it. This was a strange family. He remembered what Clio had said: Lucia was the daughter of Meg's best friend and had practically been a child when Jay went away with her to Italy. He wondered if Meg cared about that. If she did, she didn't show it. Maybe not now, because it was a long time ago, but had she cared then? He wondered what she'd felt when it had happened. Where Richard came from, she would have been 'devastated'. Like Auntie Rose next door when Uncle Jeff ran off with that woman from his work. That had been years ago, but she was still in tears more often than not.

'She'll never get over it.' That was his mother's verdict. A scandal of the very first order. Only spoken of in hushed tones, if at all. In his world, that kind of split contained more bitterness than any leaf or root that grew in the Witches' Garden. Yet here they all seemed to be the best of friends. Richard couldn't quite understand it.

Meg was going on about 'the children', her grown-up daughters Naeve and Freya, along with their current partners and exes and all the grandchildren. Richard lost track of their names after a very short time. He was not really listening. He was too busy thinking about Clio, wondering where she was.

She was probably with that Martin guy. Richard had made a special point of noticing him last night. He was young, not much older than Richard himself, with long stringy limbs which seemed to move of their own accord, giving him an odd undulating walk, like some kind of cartoon character. He had *very* bad spots, his cheeks covered in purplish lumps and pocks that he tried to disguise with tinted stuff that looked suspiciously like make-up. He was a phoney, Richard decided; why couldn't she see that? His hair was shaved in a number one and he wore high-laced Doc Martens, tight black jeans, T-shirt and braces, so he looked like a skinhead, but his earrings and accent clashed with that. Richard couldn't stand people who pretended to be something they were not. He hated the way he swaggered about with that long-lens Nikon slung like a codpiece, level with his crotch. Last night he'd been everywhere; climbing over people, showing off, drawing attention to himself, taking photographs, making little frames with his fingers, dancing about Clio like a fool. But she probably liked that. She was probably with him right now. Right this minute.

'There will be another lot here by lunchtime,' Meg was

saying. 'Friends from London. Jay's not going up to town any more, so they have to come to him.' She heaved herself up from the chair. 'No sign of Lucia. I'd better see about lunch.'

She went off towards the kitchen, her mouth drawn in a tight line. Could that be disapproval? Perhaps there was some tension there after all.

Richard rose to leave.

'No need for you to go,' she called back to him. 'Stay for lunch. Meet everybody.'

That was precisely why he'd decided to make himself scarce. Maybe he could persuade Clio to go off with him somewhere.

'Clio should be back soon. I don't know *where* she could have got to.'

Richard didn't know, either, and not knowing was adding to his restless discomfort. He didn't want to miss her, though. Wanting to see her, even for a little while, was a constant need, a craving within him, like other people have for drugs or cigarettes.

He sat on the sofa feeling more and more uncomfortable. There was still no sign of Clio. Two small children appeared in front of him, about four or five with long hair to the shoulders, both wearing grubby vests but otherwise naked. Neither spoke, just fixed him with owl-eyed stares. The boy trailed a grey matted blanket and sucked on his thumb. The other one stood exploring her nose with her right index finger.

Richard didn't know many small children. He tried smiling and saying, 'Hello, what's your name?' but got nowhere with that. So he tried staring back. They won. He closed his eyes, pretending to sleep. A damp finger poked at his cheek, then tried to worm its way into his mouth. He sat up quickly. The child's face was inches from his, a bubble of mucus emptying then filling in her crusty little nostril. Richard stood up fast.

Outside, car wheels crunched on gravel. An engine roared and died as the driver cut the ignition. Sounded powerful. More of them were arriving in fancy cars. Definitely time to go.

As he went out, he heard Clio's voice and someone answering. A man. He stood, caught between wanting to leave before she saw him and wanting to know who was talking to her.

'I don't know why Hammond lets you drive his car.' Clio was laughing. 'You drive like a maniac!'

'So?' The voice was clearer, they were coming towards him. A boy speaking. Must be Martin. 'He drives like an old lady. Shame to waste a car like that.'

Sure enough, Martin came round the corner, walking backwards, snapping pictures.

'I know a guy,' he was saying. 'Tom, they call him. He could do things for you. He's like that with all the agencies.' He held up crossed fingers. 'We should do a shoot, get a portfolio together. You've got what it takes, Clio. Trust me. I know.'

Clio was carrying a basket over one arm, filled with boxes of eggs and green-top milk. She was laughing, shaking her head.

'Don't be stupid,' she said.

'I'm serious! I can –'

Richard would have to walk past them, or go back and sit down again. Through the door, the owl-eyed children were still staring. One was perched on the sofa, a wet patch spreading all around her. Richard preferred to take his chances outside. They would probably ignore him. *He* wasn't a photographer. *He* didn't know geezers called Tom who could do things for her, who were like *that* with all the agencies. He was just a schoolboy.

'Hi, Richard.' Clio smiled when she saw him. 'Hey! Where are you going?'

'I, er, I've got to go,' he said, pushing past them.

'Who's that?' he heard Martin ask.

'That's Richard. He's a friend. Hey, Richard! Come back!'

'Really?' Martin drawled. 'I thought he was a lost Boy Scout. Dib dib dib,' he shouted as Richard turned round. Then he laughed, a high-pitched whinnying neigh, and waved limp fingers in mock salute.

Richard returned his own two-fingered version and went off down the steps.

Head of a Boy (1) (Joe)

(1960) Pencil on light brown paper
17.5 x 17.5 cm
The Dalton Estate
Jethro Arnold Dalton R.A. (1916–1976)

Head of a Boy (2) (Richard)

(1976) Charcoal and ink
29.7 x 42.0 cm
The Dalton Estate
Jethro Arnold Dalton R.A. (1916–1976)

These two studies (Plates 31, 32), one of a child, one of an adolescent, remind us that some of Dalton's very best work is to be found in the depiction of youth. These charming drawings show a suavity and freshness of vision that belie their apparent simplicity. The artist's delicate, tender execution enhances the shrewd probity in his delineation of character. The way he captures the incipient sulkiness in the boy's expression, the jittery nervousness of the adolescent, appears effortless, and that is where Dalton's power is at its greatest. He never allows the physical beauty of his subject, or their apparent innocence, to blur his clarity of view. Something of his subjects' inner lives, their characters, always shows through.

(*Dalton: A Life in Painting*, J. R. Pyne, Phaeton, London, 1980)

Richard arrived back at the Wish House in the early afternoon, just in time to see the white Sunbeam Alpine convertible turn out of the gates. Clio's hair swung, metallic in the sun. She might have glanced in his direction, but the car didn't stop, or even slow down. She carried on laughing, and talking to Hammond, who was driving. He didn't look in Richard's direction, either. His chunky watch flashed on his tanned wrist as he turned the wheel. Martin sat in the back, his legs splayed, knees jacked up, folded like paper clips. He ignored Richard, too, staring straight through him as the car swept past.

'Looking for Clio?' Joe was sitting cross-legged on the lawn, sound equipment all around him. 'You just missed her, mate. Hammond knows a bloke with a yacht at Saundersfoot. They've all gone in different cars.'

Richard didn't say that he'd seen her. It had taken a lot to swallow his pride and come back. Then to be blanked like that. Richard felt foolish.

'Jay gone, too?' Richard couldn't see him on a yacht, somehow.

'Nah.' Joe's narrow face broke into a grin. 'Can't stand boats. He's up in his studio.'

'Oh.' Richard looked around, feeling even more of a spare part.

'You can help me, if you like. I could do with another pair of hands.' He nodded at the snaking profusion of leads. 'Need to be an octopus to cope with this lot.'

'What are you doing?'

'Trying to get more sound out of these.' He tapped one of the speakers. 'I've got a new amp. Picked it up this morning. Trying to see what I can get out of it. Trouble is, I don't know if the rest of the system is going to take it.'

Richard didn't know a woofer from a tweeter, but he was willing to hold screwdrivers and plug in jack leads, not having anything better to do. They worked together without saying much.

'You like this kind of stuff?' Richard asked to break the silence.

'Yeah. Yeah, I do.' Joe looked up. His eyes were like Clio's. The same violet with long lashes. He grinned. His teeth were a little bit crooked. 'The old man sent me to college to do Art Foundation, but I was crap, not like Little Miss Picasso. Switched to Electrical Engineering. The old man thought I was mad. *He* can't even change a plug. I've worked with bands on and off, doing the sound and that. Last lot broke up. I'm kind of hanging out now, waiting to see what comes up. How about you? What do you want to do?'

'I don't know. I'm still at school.'

'OK,' Joe replied, as if that explained everything and nothing. 'Here.' He handed Richard a bunch of leads. 'Plug 'em in there, there and there.' Richard followed Joe's instructions. 'Now we're ready to go.' Joe levered himself up from the floor. Anything you'd like to hear?'

'Got any Cream?'

Joe wound a long extension lead into the house.

'Any special track?'

'"Strange Brew"?' Richard asked, remembering this morning.

'A lad after my own heart!' Joe's smile flashed. He flicked his long hair back. When he grinned like that, he looked disturbingly like his sister. 'I like that track, too. You've got it!'

The opening chords crashed out. Richard was sitting next to the bass speaker. The deep sound came out so loud, it shook the ground, vibrating right through him.

'How about that?' Joe came dancing back. 'Cool, or what?'

The track ended in a fierce clash of guitars and crackled into 'I Feel Free'. Richard hummed and clapped, and then began drumming on the wooden edge of the speaker, while Joe leaped around the garden, singing along, playing air guitar.

'What the hell is going on?' A window flew out above them, Jay stuck his head out. 'For Christ's sake, Joe! Turn the bloody thing off! I'm trying to work up here. I can't hear myself think!'

The window slammed shut. Joe waited until the track had finished and went back into the house.

'Too much distortion anyway,' he said, as he came back. 'Need to get the treble up somehow.'

The window above them opened again.

'That Richard with you?' Jay's voice sounded loud in the sudden silence of the garden. 'I want to see him. Come up here.'

Richard rose, ready to obey his command.

Joe looked up from where he'd begun stripping cable. 'What does he want you for? Does he want you to pose?'

Richard nodded. He suddenly felt nervous. His mouth dry, his legs hollow.

'Where exactly is his studio?' He hadn't been up there before.

'Up the stairs, turn left. Through the trapdoor.'

'Right.'

'There's a tribe some place –' Joe twisted the strands of bright wire between his thin, strong fingers – 'South America? Africa?' He shrugged as if where didn't really matter. 'They believe to take a likeness is to steal a soul. You be careful. He used to paint me all the time when I was young.'

Jay pulled the ladder up hand over hand with a length of rope. The trapdoor went down with a thump.

'Repel boarders.' Jay laughed at the look on Richard's face. 'Don't look so worried! I'm not planning to have my wicked way with you. I don't like to be disturbed when I'm working, that's all.'

A series of skylights had been set into the north-facing side of the roof, giving that part of the room a different, fragile quality, like a conservatory. Light fell in slanting blocks, bringing a soft sheen to the dark polished floorboards. Paint had been dripped, spattered and smeared all over the place. Ruining a nice floor like that. Richard's mother would have had a fit. A big old-fashioned shiny brass telescope stood by the open window, swivelled to point out to sea. A long hank of seaweed, hanging from the window latch, gave off a faint scent of ammonia as the fronds crinkled in the heat.

Two large easels had been set at angles to a long trestle table formed from an old door resting on a couple of struts. Next to the place where the artist stood, the surface was crusted with miniature mountain ranges of paint. Twisted, mangled dull metal tubes oozed colour and different-sized brushes lay heaped like pick-up sticks. A couple of wide-mouthed, tide-marked jars stood next to a cluster of cork-stoppered bottles containing oily turps and golden linseed oil, their ridged glass hazed and fingerprinted with paint.

Sketches and drawings lay in scattered drifts, and the floor beneath the table was littered with nests of crumpled rags, stained and stiff like discarded dressings.

One easel held a big canvas covered with a sheet; Richard guessed it to be the portrait of Clio. He would have loved to have taken a peek, but he didn't even ask to see it. He knew without being told that such a request would be refused.

The other canvas was blank.

'Have you had lunch?'

'No,' Richard answered, mystified, wondering if the artist was about to offer him something.

He wasn't.

'Good. I don't want your belly sticking out like a plush monkey. Don't look so worried.' The artist gave a wheezing laugh. 'You don't have to drop your kecks for me, lad. Just take your top off. That'll do. Now, stand over there.'

Richard did as he was told.

'No.' The artist changed his mind. 'Sit on the stool. Not like that. More relaxed. Don't slump! You look like a puppet with the strings cut. Keep your back straight. Arms down. No. One hand on your knee. Look away. No. Look at me.'

The artist prowled around him, barking out instructions, manipulating and changing his position until he was satisfied. He moved close, then closer, looking and peering from different angles. Then he stepped back and stood very still, hand resting on his chin. His eyes seemed to widen and narrow again, like the aperture of a camera lens.

'That's better. That's all right. Now don't move.' He didn't go back to his easel, but dragged out an old paint-stained kitchen chair from under the table. He groped for charcoal and pad without taking his eyes off Richard.

'Don't turn! Just as you were! That's right. That's nice. Don't move an inch. Not a muscle. Not until I tell you.'

He sat, left ankle resting on right knee. He was left-handed, Richard noticed, with thick wrists and strong arms for a man of his age. He settled the pad across his lap and began to sketch, hardly speaking again until the session was ended. A fly buzzed, banging against a windowpane again and again. The only other sounds were the noise the charcoal made as Jay drew it across the paper and the rubbing of his thumb as he blurred the lines. A steel nib scratched and screeched as he switched to pen and ink. Paper ripped and buckled as sheet after sheet was torn from the pad. The artist hissed through his teeth and muttered as each piece sifted down from his lap to the floor.

Every little movement Richard made was noted, and scolded; otherwise the artist ignored him. A deep bass thud-thudding pulsed up from beneath. Joe had got his stereo going. Richard tried to spot the track while he waited for the artist to bawl him out again. He didn't seem to hear, or to see anything except Richard and the paper in front of him.

'That's it.'

The artist stopped drawing and let the pad slide off his knees on to the floor. He looked tired. Eyes closed. His face drained. Richard was feeling pretty tired himself. Strange how being still for so long could take it out of you, he thought as he pulled on his T-shirt.

'See you the same time tomorrow.' Jay's eyes fluttered open. 'Bring the togs you were wearing that first day.'

The day was still hot, the sky bright white, but Richard was surprised how much time had passed when he looked at his watch.

126

'How's it going?'

Joe was still fiddling with his stereo system. 'Get this!' He pushed a button and sound boomed out.

'That's great!'

'Yeah. All balanced up and nothing's blown yet.' He pulled his thin black shirt away from his narrow chest. He was wearing old blue jeans, slung low at the hip, cut off above the knees. 'It's hot. Fancy a swim?'

'I don't have any trunks with me.'

Joe snorted. 'You don't need 'em. No one else will be wearing any.'

'No one else?' Robert felt his heart jolt. 'Clio?'

'Been back ages. They're all down at the beach.'

'What about the yacht?'

'Hammond got the tides wrong. Guy had already gone. Just going to grab a towel. You coming, Rick?'

'Got to get back.' Richard turned to go. 'Some other time.'

'Yeah. You coming up tomorrow?'

'I guess.' Richard's glance went to the attic windows.

'See you, then. And thanks for your help, man.' Joe clasped Richard's hand.

'Yeah, see you.' Richard returned his grip, pleased to be called Rick.

'What are you doing, Richard?' His mother called from outside as Richard opened and shut cupboards.

'Looking for Dad's binoculars.'

'What do you want them for?'

'Birdwatching.' It was only half a lie. 'Dylan says there's a falcon nesting in the cliff up past Hope's Bay.'

'You're not going out again?' She was standing at the door now, watching. 'I was just thinking about tea.'

'What are we having?' Richard could see no signs of food preparation.

'Sandwiches. I thought sandwich spread would be nice. Something light. It's too hot for anything else.'

'I'm not hungry.'

Sandwich spread was disgusting. Salad cream full of bits and it looked like sick. The binoculars were hanging from a hook in the closet, behind Dad's all-weather jacket.

'I'll be back later.' He had gone before she could make any other objections.

He lay on the cliff looking down at them spread out like a desert tribe on a patchwork of towels and blankets. He searched for Clio, but couldn't see her. He was relieved not to find her there because most of them were naked, like Joe had said. He knew it was wrong of him, but he didn't want to see her like that. Not on public view. He found Martin, rubbing oil into Hammond's tanned back. Lucia was doing the same for Joe. He swung the binoculars back. An empty towel lay near the two men. Someone was missing. Could be a threesome. Jealousy nagged at him. Could be Clio.

He surveyed the rest of the group. Meg and daughters, grandchildren excavating huge craters and making sand-castles much nearer to the adult encampment than his mother would ever allow. They were so unlike his own family. Anyone he knew. So loud, for one thing. Their voices carried all the way back here. They seemed totally unconscious of everyone else around. They never told each other to keep their voices down. They didn't hop round in circles, trying to jab a foot through a pair of underpants while getting dressed inside a towel. They didn't care who saw what, or what anyone thought of them.

They were so much at ease together, rubbing oil on to

each other's bodies. His family didn't even use it; they just burned bright red. That's what they called it, sunburn, not suntan. Lucia and Meg especially didn't seem to be able to talk to anyone without holding on to them, as if that was a vital part of the conversation. They treated each other with an intimacy which seemed totally natural, but was unimaginable in the world that Richard knew.

'Nothing hidden. Nothing forbidden.' Wasn't that what Lucia had said?

They talked endlessly about everything. Unlike in his own family where silence was golden and everything went on below a shiny blank surface, like a Formica breakfast bar patterned with a facsimile of modern family life.

'What are you doing up here?'

He must have fallen asleep. He woke with a start to find Clio leaning over him, her wrap falling open. She was naked underneath.

'Spying. I see.' She picked up the binoculars. 'What's the point of that? Why don't you come down and join us?'

She rolled over, training the binoculars at the party down below her.

'Hey! This is interesting!' She laughed. 'Like a programme I saw about a colony of apes, in Japan I think it was. They lived by the sea. Why did you go off this morning?'

'Because you were with that guy.'

'Which guy?' Clio asked sharply.

'Martin.' Richard did not want to look at her. Her change of tone had to admit some kind of guilt. 'Then this afternoon, you went off with him in the car.'

'Martin!' She sounded surprised. 'You mustn't be jealous of Martin.' She continued to look through the binoculars. 'He's all talk. He doesn't know anyone in the fashion business. He's just a student. It's a joke between us. Besides, he's not interested in me.'

'Oh, really?' Richard said quietly. 'How could any boy not be?'

'Well. *He* isn't. He's my nephew, for one thing. Well, half-nephew, or some kind of nephew-in-law.'

'*Nephew?*' How could that be?

'My family's complicated. I told you. He's Naeve's ex-partner's eldest son. And he's gay, for another thing. Or he thinks he is.'

'He's *queer?*' Richard took the binoculars off her. 'Let me see. How doesn't he know?' He adjusted the focus. 'You either are, or you aren't, I would have thought.'

'It's not always as easy as that. Not everyone's like you. He's after Charles Hammond.'

'The one with the Che tash? But he's old! Don't tell me he's one, too!'

Clio shrugged, her eyes clouded, enigmatic. 'What do you mean?'

'You know, a poofter.' Richard studied them carefully. 'I've never seen real ones before.'

'Don't talk like that.' She took the binoculars away from him. 'They aren't animals in a zoo.'

'You introduced the idea.' Richard rolled over to look at her. 'Is he?'

'No, I don't think so.' She was looking through the binoculars again. 'Although he spends a lot of time in Morocco. He's an old friend of Jay's, or used to be. He was his pupil. Went into advertising, made pots of money. He's a dealer now. Owns a gallery. Wants some paintings off Jay, and Jay won't sell. Jay doesn't much like dealers. Calls them piranhas. He thinks Hammond has sold out.'

Richard wasn't much interested in that.

'What do you mean?' he asked. 'About Morocco. Are they all, you know, out there?'

'Homosexuality is accepted as something quite natural, if that's what you mean. I don't want you to talk about it like that. Anyway, I'm almost completely certain Hammond isn't.'

'How can you be so sure?' Richard asked, out of interest more than anything. Even his suspicions did not run to old men.

'He was Lucia's lover for a while. And –'

'And what?'

'He was Lucia's lover. Isn't that enough?' Clio continued to stare through the binoculars. 'He wouldn't be interested in Martin anyway.'

'Why not?'

'Because he's too ugly. Which is why I wouldn't be, either.' She took the binoculars away from her eyes, reversing them. 'How small you are. Small but perfectly formed.'

'But Jay and Lucia.' Richard rolled away, not wanting to be teased by her. 'They're married to each other. They seem happy together. Why . . .?'

She sighed and put the binoculars aside. 'Why do they take other lovers? Why do you care?'

'Because I don't understand.'

'Why do you have to understand everything? They are different, that's all. They lead a different kind of life. Why can't you accept it? Besides, it's not really your business, so why worry about it?' Richard felt he'd been told off, admonished, but she took his hand, drawing him over to her. 'Don't look like that. I know.' She rose to her feet, pulling him after her. 'Let's go somewhere a bit more private.'

*

'Do you want to go on seeing me?' she said, as they lay together in the place they'd found in the dunes.

'Of course I do!' Richard looked over to her, her eyes were level with his.

'Well you're going to have to stop being so possessive and jealous.' She took a curl of his hair, twisting it round her finger. 'I can't stand that. When there are people here, I have to stay and help Lucia. Besides that, they are my family. I can't be with you exclusively.' She stood up, winding herself back into her wrap. 'Come down with me.' She held out a hand to pull him up after her. 'Get to know everybody. You'll like them, once you get to know them.'

Richard went with her, although he still did not want to share her. He wanted her for himself. That desire was like a fire within him, but he was good at hiding it. He'd been hiding things all his life.

Knave of Batons
Waite Pack

Traditional appearance: A youth standing
out of doors, holding an upright club with
both hands. He is shown in profile, wearing
a short tunic with a knee-length cloak
over it. On his head is a floppy cap.

Divinatory meanings:
upright: He is ambitious and resourceful,
enthusiastic and adaptable. He is a
messenger who brings good tidings,
stimulating news, witty gossip. He is by
nature faithful and trustworthy, vigorous
in the service of those in authority over
him.

Reversed: He brings misleading information
and slanderous gossip, and propagates
scandal. He is unable to keep a secret and
will readily betray his trust. He is
superficial whilst believing himself to be
profound.

(*The Tarot*, Alfred Douglas, Victor Gollancz, 1974)

Tarot Card stuck in Clio Dalton's notebook with
divinatory meanings (August, 1976).
Followed by RICHARD (underlined three times)

If he wanted her, if he wanted to be with her, he had to become part of the shifting community that centred round Jay and his wife. Clio made that clear. It was proving to be an exceptional summer and visitors came and stayed, kept there by the succession of long, hot days, the beauty of the place. Not just the family. Lucia and Jay had lots of friends: students past and present, fellow artists, thin girls in wispy dresses accompanied by young men dressed in black, long-haired hippie types, older, bearded blokes in little steel-rimmed glasses who came trailing pregnant wives and hordes of children. Richard watched them come and go in a parade of old cars, post office vans and VW campers. Sometimes there was not enough room, so they slept on the floor, camped in the garden or down on the beach, or took houses in the village.

Every afternoon was spent on the beach. Richard began to learn not to be self-conscious and bathed naked like everyone else. His hair bleached in the relentless sunlight and his skin turned golden all over. He looked forward to explaining that in the showers at school.

There was a price to pay for being included in this end-less house party. Richard had to spend a portion of each day posing for Jay.

He had to wear the same clothes that he'd worn on that first day.

'Relax,' the painter said. 'I don't want you all stiff like a mannequin just because we're going to start painting. What did I tell you before? No, no, no.' He shook his head at

135

Richard's efforts to comply. 'You look like a girl who wants to go the lavvy. Here.'

Jay came over to move him. This was far more rigorous than when Jay had just been doing sketches. Richard felt strong hands wrenching him about, pulling, pushing him into position as if he was some kind of bendy rubber toy.

'That's better.' Jay stood back, stroking his beard, fixing Richard with his camera stare again. 'That's all right. Now stay like that. It's all in the looking. Artists look differently. Use their eyes properly. Remember that, lad. You have to look carefully if you want to really see.'

This explanation was the only one the artist ever gave to Richard for putting him through real discomfort. He felt impossibly stretched, his stance hopelessly unnatural. His muscles were aching already. He was sure he wouldn't be able to stay like this for more than a couple of seconds, let alone hours. Clio had warned him that portrait sessions could go on for a long time.

'How long?' he had asked.

'As long as he wants you.'

Still the artist did not start. He studied Richard, his black eyes dull and matt, his forehead scissored into a deep frown. The more he stared, the more exposed Richard felt. Knowing he would not have to pose nude had been reassuring, but now it didn't seem to matter that he did have clothes on. It was as if Jay could see right through to the skin, beneath that even. Richard felt flayed by his gaze, put in a place beyond embarrassment.

Jay's eyes flared, his brow cleared.

'That's it! That's the look I want!'

He went to the easel and began blocking out the canvas,

sketching in Richard's figure. He worked quickly, without speaking, until Richard was dismissed with a curt 'That's enough for today.'

Jay was painting all the time, working like a man driven: Clio in the morning, Richard in the afternoon. Sometimes he painted all night, Clio said; they could hear him shuffling about, pacing up and down when it didn't go right. Lucia was worried, but she would not try to stop him. Jay always did what he wanted. Nothing was allowed to interfere with his work.

The sessions were intense. Richard never got used to posing, not the way Clio was. He always found it uncomfortable. Part of the reason for that was physical, because of the way he had to stand and keep the exact same pose for what seemed like hours, but their times together could be disturbing in other ways, too.

Sometimes Jay talked, asked Richard questions. Sometimes he worked in silence.

'Don't your parents mind you spending so much time up here?'

It was a question that Lucia had asked him several times. Richard had begun to worry that he was outstaying his welcome, but Clio said no, Lucia was just concerned in case his parents were missing him. That had made Richard smile. His dad went off fishing every day and didn't particularly want to take Richard. His mother couldn't wait to see the back of him. He could see her, curled up on her lounger.

'For God's sake, Richard.' She wouldn't even take her eyes from the page she was reading. 'Find something to do, can't you? And stop hanging about.'

'No,' Richard replied when Jay asked. He'd learned not

137

to shake his head. 'Mum says it's the best holiday she's ever had. Holidays are to do what you like, that's what she says, and she likes doing nothing. Sits outside the 'van, reading on the lounger. She suffers from her nerves, you see,' he offered by way of explanation. 'Needs the rest.'

Richard suspected her tiredness and indifference had more to do with the tablets she was taking, although when she didn't take them she was anxious and irritable, which was actually a whole lot worse. Richard and his dad would rather put up with how she was now than the other thing: the constant worrying about nothing, the upsets and mood swings, but he didn't feel like explaining his entire family history to Jay. Anyway, the last thing he wanted at the moment was for her to take too much interest in where he was, what he was doing. She'd only start interfering.

'What does she think you do all day?'

'She thinks I'm with Dylan.'

'The lad from the farm?' Jay gave a rusty laugh. 'The one that shares an interest in horticulture with Lucia?'

'That's him.'

'He's offered to show her a couple of local rarities.' Jay laughed again. 'She's *very* excited.'

Richard thought he knew what was going on there and had to resist a desire to smile. After the barbecue, Dylan had found it hard to get his head round the idea of Richard and Clio together, but he wasn't one to mope, or bear grudges. He'd gone after the mother. She had been impressed by his knowledge of local flora. She must have taken up his offer to show her some of the sites of special interest. 'Botanical seduction,' Dylan called it.

He hadn't seen Dylan for a while. He wondered how far he'd got in his campaigning. Did Jay know what else might be going on? How much did he care if it was? If he *did* care, the one he ought to be keeping an eye on was Hammond. He always seemed to be there when Richard came down from his session.

'What about your dad?'

'What?'

'You're here. Your mum's on the lounger. What does your dad do all day?'

'He goes fishing.'

'And you don't like fishing?'

'Depends. I don't mind fishing from the beach, or from a breakwater, or rocks, but Dad likes to go out with a guy from the village who's got a boat. I don't like boats. Get sea-sick on a lake.'

'You prefer to spend your time up here with us. With Clio?'

'Yes, I guess.' Richard felt himself blush.

'So you're responsible for all the bruises down her back?'

Richard blushed even harder.

'She seems to like you.'

Richard did not know what to reply to that. Conversation died away between them. He felt the intense, blue-black gaze pass over him. He was not supposed to move in any way, or turn his head. Nevertheless, he could feel when the artist's eyes were on him. Sometimes the sensation was almost physical, like a scraping away of his skin.

Sometimes they didn't speak at all until the curt 'That's enough for today' dismissed him. Other times, like today, Jay was more talkative. Richard's ability to reply was limited by the posing, making these conversations rather one-sided. Anyway, he didn't always understand exactly what the artist was talking about.

'Transience is the artist's tragedy,' Jay went on after a long period of silence. 'Artists often collect. Sometimes compulsively. They hang on to things. They don't want to let go. Like paintings. I don't want to part with them. Some I won't sell at any price. I don't even let people see 'em.'

The paintings were stored in racks that extended all along one side of the room. Most of the slots were occupied. Richard had speculated about what these racks contained. Now he wondered what was so special about these paintings kept only for private view. It made no sense to him. How could an artist make a living without selling his paintings? It seemed an odd thing to do.

'Why not?' he asked. 'Surely that's the whole point.'

'Why?' Dalton's eyes were fierce. 'Not for them to see. Eyes front!' he snapped. 'Stop swivelling about!' Even the slightest movement made him irritable. Richard did as he was told. 'If I do sell a painting, I often have to paint it again. For me. Do you see?'

Richard didn't.

'How do you make any money,' he asked, 'if you don't sell your paintings? Who pays for everything?'

Laughter rumbled deep in Jay's chest.

'I didn't say I never sold *any*. I sell enough. It's not just me. Others do it, too. We don't like change and we are possessive. Maybe that's why we do it. We want to hang on to things. Hang on to the one time. We don't want to let it go. We want to capture it. Keep it forever. Or one person. How they were then. At that moment. That's what I want. To stop time. To have that power.' Richard felt the bruise-black eyes taking him in and tried not to shiver at the prickling on his skin. 'You have already changed. Your skin is a shade or two darker, and your hair is longer, and lighter because of the sun.' Jay was always grumbling about his skin tones changing and his hair bleaching. Richard was not going to give up his time on the beach for art. He was

140

having too much fun there. 'You're still growing, so you'll be a tiny bit taller, your limbs longer. You've probably changed in other ways.' His careful scrutiny suddenly took on a piercing intensity. 'So the garden in the painting, the house in the background, what it contains, these things are no longer there for you to discover. Change, you see?'

'But keeping things always the same is impossible.'

'I know.' Jay went back to his painting. 'Doesn't stop me wanting it, though. Don't you ever want anything impossible, Richard?'

'I don't know . . .' Richard mumbled, aware that his private dreams of playing football for the Villa, being in a band, just vaguely being famous, would sound trivial and frivolous.

'Yes, you do.' Jay put down his brush. 'You want girls like Clio to love you.' He took up the rag he kept to wipe his hands. Richard smelt the turpentine. 'That's enough for today. You can go.'

Girl with Yellow Shawl

(1955) Oil on canvas
76.2 x 101.62 cm
Tate Gallery
Jethro Arnold Dalton R.A. (1916–1976)

The model for this nude was Lucy (later Lucia) Ivanoff, the
artist's second wife. She is the subject of the intense observa-
tion that is so typical of Dalton's work at this time: his hyper-
realist style and meticulous attention to detail. Objects in the
room, the rug on the floor, the silk of the shawl, the flesh and
the hair of the model, are equally scrutinized and rendered in
a way that serves both to reveal and disguise. The viewer's eye
is both attracted to, and distracted away from, the girl on the
bed. The way the artist plays with the viewer's gaze gives this
painting its haunting, erotic power.

('Gaze and Gender', A. Price, in *Radical Revision: Essays in Popular Culture*.
eds A. Price and J. Stanley, Pandora Press, London, 1980)

Sometimes, the painting did not go so well.

The next day's session was terminated almost as soon as it had begun. Jay held his brush up, hesitating, then he brought it down again. He did this again, and again, bringing the brush down with two hands gripping, as if it was an effort, as though there was some kind of life or force bound up in the wood, like a hazel wand, or a divining rod. Finally, the brush snapped in his hands. He threw the two halves down and began pacing around, swearing. Finally he returned to the table, banging two fists down, making things bounce and topple. A jar smashed on the floor, spilling liquid. Richard tried not to flinch and kept his pose, staying as still as possible. He thought that Jay was angry, but when the artist finally turned to him his eyes were brimming with tears.

'Can't do it today, boy.' He held his hands in front of him, right clutching left. 'You'd better go.'

Richard did not need any more prompting. He was gone in seconds, sliding on the descending ladder to get down faster, relieved to be out of there, revelling in the idea of more time with Clio. The ladder was pulled up as soon as he was off it and the trapdoor went down with a thump.

He slipped into the bathroom to change out of his shorts and shirt. Aertex and khaki were strictly for the portrait. He pulled on his jeans. He'd cut them off at the knees, much to his mother's horror. 'What are you doing?' she'd screeched, in a way that reminded Richard of the time before she took her tablets. 'Those are perfectly good trousers! Years of wear in them!' That was not strictly true, because Richard kept on growing, but he did not say anything, just shrugged and carried on fraying the denim. He wanted them to look like Joe's. He'd adapted other parts of his wardrobe: tearing the necks of his T-shirts, stamping down the backs of his tennis shoes.

He went downstairs, expecting to find Clio, but there was no one about.

'Oh, hello!'

He turned fast, thinking it was Clio, but it was Lucia. They sometimes sounded just like each other. His quick smile died.

'Not Clio, I'm afraid.' Lucia laughed. 'Sorry to disappoint you. Have you finished already?'

'He told me to go. Where's Clio?'

'There was a problem this morning. Jay upset her. She went off somewhere.'

Lucia held her hands, palms up in a 'you know what she's like' kind of way. Richard nodded, as if he understood. She could be a bit unpredictable. Not always there when he finished his session, not turning up when they had arranged to meet. He'd learned not to question her about it. After her warning, he obeyed the rules.

'I thought Jay might be better behaved with you. Obviously not.' Lucia picked up the hem of her long skirt and made for the stairs. 'I ought to go and see –'

'He's pulled up the drawbridge.'

'Oh, *has* he? He'll have to stew then, won't he? Why don't you stay and wait for Clio. She won't be long, I'm certain. Sit down. It's too hot outside even for me. I'll make us some mint tea.'

They drank the tea out of little glasses.

'Good?' Lucia asked him.

'Umm,' Richard savoured the sweet minted liquid. 'Different. Nice, though.'

Lucia smiled. 'I'm glad you like it. It's very cooling in this hot weather.' She held her glass with the tips of her fingers and took a delicate sip before setting it down. 'How do you like being painted? Strange, isn't it?' Richard nodded. 'Does he ask you lots of questions?' Richard nodded again. 'He likes to do that. He likes to get close to the sitter.'

'What was he like? When he was young, I mean?'

'I don't know.' Lucia laughed. 'I didn't know him then. First time I met him I was ten and he was thirty-four. I can show you a picture, though.' She stood up and went over to a bookshelf piled with books and magazines stacked horizontally. 'There was a retrospective a couple of years ago. That's a special kind of exhibition,' she offered by way of explanation. 'Looking back over an artist's life so far. There's a catalogue somewhere. Here we are.'

She pulled out a thick, slightly dog-eared brochure, starting an avalanche of others which she ignored. She flipped through the pages as she came back.

'There he is.'

She sat next to Richard on the sofa and held the book flat for him to see. Richard leaned over, drawing closer. His curiosity had been growing deeper with each sitting. They were together for hours every day. The artist now knew all there was to know about him, but Richard knew almost nothing about Jay. He gripped the corner of the book now, bending the pages in his eagerness to see what he had been like. The first shock was that he was beardless, his cheeks and chin marked by blue shadow. Richard hadn't realized how much the beard acted as a mask. Richard studied the face intently. The mouth was finely moulded and full-lipped; it made him look vulnerable and very young. That was the second shock. For a moment Richard thought he was looking at Joe. The same wide brow, high cheekbones and narrow jaw. Thick black hair flopped down over his high forehead. The eyes were large, lustrous, and dark, like a hawk's, sharper and far more predatory than Joe's vague, violet gaze.

'He looks like Joe.'

Lucia smiled. 'He was about the same age when he painted that.'

She flipped on through the book. The pages fell open at a nude of a young woman.

'Guess who that is.'

Girl with Yellow Shawl (1955).

Richard didn't have to. So naked. So beautiful. So unsettlingly like Clio. Richard shifted in his seat, troubled by Lucia's proximity.

'I was sixteen.' Lucia leaned back, the book open on her knee. 'A little older than Clio. My parents are both artists. My mother is a potter, my father does etching, illustration. They set up a community with other artists in deepest Wiltshire.'

'Do they live there now?' Richard asked.

'No.' Lucia shook her head. 'Moved to Cornwall years ago.'

'How did you meet Jay?'

'Meg was a friend of my mother's. They had been at school together. She and the children joined the community. Jay used to come down at weekends.'

'What was he like?' Richard wanted to know more than a portrait could show him.

'Electric. Charismatic. He had this *starry* quality. He

was a dish, that was the word I think we used then.' Her face softened and her eyes shone as if she was as young as the girl in the picture. 'You knew when he'd come into a room. He had a certain way of looking that made people want to be noticed by him, want to please him. Apart from that, he was . . . elusive. His visits were infrequent, erratic. Sometimes he'd come down –' she shrugged, her face shadowed by a distant disappointment, '– sometimes he wouldn't. He didn't like to stay away from London for long. Then, out of the blue, he decided he'd had enough of the city and wanted to work in peace and quiet.' She glanced down at the book on her knee. 'He'd painted me before, but not like that.'

'What did you think?'

'I was terrified.' She laughed. 'But he made it easy. He can be surprisingly gentle. The first couple of sessions he didn't paint at all, just wanted to know me, put me at ease with myself, my body, and with him. It was rather beautiful. He managed to create a deep intimacy between us that was not at all sexual. That came later. It was amazing. I shed everyday normality with my clothes. He made me feel extraordinary. He seemed to see into the core of me. This intense, intense stare, looking closer, and closer . . . but you know, don't you?' Richard nodded, he'd felt that stare, too. 'He called me his muse. Clio is named after one of the Muses, did she tell you?' Richard shook his head. 'In the end, we went away together. It caused something of an upset at the time, but it's all fine now.' She turned more pages to reveal more nude studies. 'He hasn't painted me for years. Mirror, mirror on the wall . . .' She smiled and Richard could see the fine lines round her eyes. 'He has a different muse now.'

A car sounded in the silence that fell between them.

Coming down the lane. Richard caught the note of the engine. It was the Alpine.

The car came to a halt outside the house. A door slammed and the car pulled away again, wheels crunching the gravel.

'That's probably Clio. You are such a sweet boy, Ricardo.' She reached up and touched his cheek. 'It's nice for Clio to be with someone her own age. I hope she doesn't hurt you too much.'

'You're out early,' Clio said as she came in.

'Who was that?'

'Hammond. I met him in town. He gave me a lift back.'

'Not coming in?' Lucia sounded disappointed.

'Had to get back to London. He'll be down at the week-end with those people you invited.'

'Oh, God! I'd completely forgotten. And with Jay like this . . .' Lucia sighed and her face tightened. Lines of strain showed at the sides of her mouth and her blue eyes looked suddenly tired. 'Perhaps I should try to cancel . . .'

'You can't do that!' Clio sounded outraged. 'It wouldn't be good manners. He might be all right by then. Besides, I thought they were old artist friends of Jay's. They might provide a diversion. Take his mind off his problems.'

'You could be right.' Lucia's brow cleared and she kissed her daughter. 'Wise beyond your years. I've got a hamper ready for the beach. Meg's down there with Naeve and the children. I thought we might have a picnic. You two can take it down for me.'

'This'll do.' Clio found a place in the dunes. 'Now what have we got here?' She flipped open the lid of the hamper. 'Yum, yum! Roast chicken and cherry cake. A real beach feast. Ooh, look! Lemonade!' She waved the bottle. 'How thoughtful of Lucia. That must be for you.'

'Hang on!' Richard tried to stop her grabbing things. 'Isn't this supposed to be for everybody?'

'Never mind about them. I don't know about you, but I'm starving. They can have the leftovers.'

'What are they going to think when we turn up with a stack of bones and a pile of crumbs?'

'Who cares?'

'But it's not right!'

'That's the trouble with you, Richard. You are always worrying about what other people think and what's right or not. What if there isn't a right thing, have you ever thought of that? They aren't exactly going to starve to death, are they? You've got to learn to be more selfish. Here –' she held up a chicken leg for him to bite. 'You can see it as your reward for carrying it down.' Richard bit into the meat, tearing at the sweet flesh with his teeth. 'That's more like it!'

Clio laughed, plundering the hamper for more food to feed him, throwing the chicken bones at the gathering gulls.

Jay's I Ching

Hexagram 36 – Ming I: Darkening of the light

TRIGRAMS

Upper: K'un – Earth
Nether: Li – Fire
Nuclear: Chen – Thunder (above)
K'an – Water (below)

Earth over fire – as in the sun sinking under the earth and being darkened. Name means: brightness wounded.

THE LINES:

[from bottom]

1. [He] flies with drooping wings. When the wise man is resolving his going away, he may not eat for three days. Wherever he goes, the people deride him.

2. [He] is wounded in the left thigh. [He] saves himself by the strength of a swift horse. Fortunate.

3. [He] hunts in the south and takes the great chief of darkness. [He] should not be eager to make all correct at once.

4. [He] enters into the left side of the belly of the dark land, but is able to quit the gate and the courtyard of the land of darkness.

5. [He] does his duty. It will be advantageous to be firm and correct.
6. There is no light, only darkness. [He] first climbed to heaven, but his future shall be to go into the depths of the earth.

INAUSPICIOUS!

(Jay's I Ching, 25/8/76 – Lucia's notebook)

The Wish House Summer was moving through phases, just like the moon. When Richard first met Clio, the moon had been a thin sliver of silver, bright enough for the old moon to show in ghostly filigree. Now it was moving towards the full, hanging in the sky like a burnished, brazen gong, mountains and seas stippling the surface.

By the weekend, Meg and her daughters had moved on to another friend's house further down the coast after Meg'd had some kind of argument with Jay. What about? Clio had no idea.

'She's the only one who's not scared of him,' she said. 'Probably got fed up with him being so grumpy.'

There were a lot of other people for dinner. There was enough light to eat out of doors, but Lucia decided that there were too many mosquitoes about and no one could be bothered to move the furniture. The seating arrangements were haphazard, and Richard found himself right down the far end of the table, nowhere near Clio. She was sitting near the head of the table, between Hammond and her mother. Lucia had to keep getting up and doing things: seeing to the cooking, bringing in dishes, fetching more wine from the larder. Clio did not seem too interested in helping her and was deep in conversation with the art dealer. Richard strained his ears, trying to hear what they were talking about, but he could pick up almost nothing. His end of the table was dominated by Martin.

Martin had arrived from London wearing a stained white T-shirt displaying a torn Union Jack further embellished with various slogans attached by nappy pins and bulldog clips. His bitten fingernails were painted black and his tight trousers had zips all over, quite apart from the usual places. No one commented on his outfit, although where Richard came from they would have dismembered him for disfiguring the flag like that. They were sitting with Joe and a couple of student types Richard didn't really know. Joe was friendly enough but the others ignored him. They were listening to Martin.

'It's dead, I'm telling you, man.' Martin helped himself to more red wine, over-filling his glass so the wine pooled and spread along the grooves of the scrubbed wood table. 'Drawing. Painting. Waste of time. That's why I took up photography.'

'You are such a bullshitter!' Joe laughed and shook his head. 'You took up photography because you were crap at the other stuff. You were even worse than me.'

'*Not* the point!' Martin jabbed a nicotine-stained finger at Joe. 'Things are changing. He's had it, if you ask me.' He jerked his thumb at Jay, who was sitting with a couple of older artists. 'His sort of art is dead. The corpse is already beginning to rot.' He waved a hand. 'Here we see the flies gathering.' He leaned forward on the table. 'Nah, the future doesn't lie with him. It's with that bloke who put the bricks in the Tate.'

'Carl Andre's *Equivalent VIII*?' someone supplied.

'That's the one. That's the future. Not all this painting bollocks! Waste of time –'

Jay's place was at the head of the table. The people around him were deep in serious talk but Jay did not join in. He sat listening, stroking his beard, his lips twitching to a half-smile, dark eyes shifting from face to face. Martin's voice was rising, cutting through the other conversations.

Hammond shot him a warning look which just made him louder.

Suddenly, Jay stood up. A movement unexpected enough to quieten those nearest to him. Silence spread down the table. Martin was the last to stop talking. All faces turned towards the artist, but he said nothing. His eyes went from one person to another, as though assessing their worth to him. He shook his head slightly, as if he found them all wanting, then he pushed his chair back and made for the stairs.

Lucia went after him. Conversation surged back in a nervous, hurried rush. Loud, but not loud enough for the guests to miss Jay's instruction to Lucia to get rid of them. Now wouldn't be soon enough.

Lucia came back, fixed smile in place.

'Don't mind him. He's a bit pissed,' she announced as she made her way round to Clio. She put a hand on her daughter's shoulder, whispering in her ear. Clio rose and went to the stairs; the rest looked to Lucia. She gestured that everything was all right, for them to get on with their meal.

'He's been overworking,' she added, as if that explained everything. 'It's all fine!' She sighed as she moved past Richard's chair, muttering, 'I feel like Lady Macbeth.'

He stood up, offering to help.

'Not much you can do.' She gave him a wan smile. 'It's not going to improve. I'd get off home, if I were you.'

'I'd better say goodbye to Clio,' he said.

'No need.'

'But I was going to stay. She might wonder . . .'

'I'll tell her that you've gone. She'll understand. Come on.' She put her arm around his waist, shepherding him to

157

the door. 'I've sent her up to calm him. It might take a while. See you tomorrow, Ricardo, *cara mio*.'

The heavy wooden door shut behind him. Richard stood outside, watching the lights of the house come on in different combinations. The studio was lit end to end. Jay must have gone up there, Clio following. Perhaps he was painting her. No. A light went on in Clio's room. She came to the window to draw the curtains. Richard started up, meaning to go over and attract her attention, then he held back and stayed cloaked in shadow. There was a dark shape behind her. Someone else with her. Maybe Jay had followed her down to talk to her. The curtains closed. Light showed though the red fabric like a flame through a membrane.

He went close to the house again. Through the window, he could see Joe and Martin sprawled at opposite ends of the sofa, other people lying about on cushions. Some were sucking on pipes, others passing round a spliff the size of a large root vegetable. No sign of Lucia. Or Hammond. Lights had come on in the room Lucia shared with Jay. Maybe he was up there with her. Clio's light had gone off now. She must be alone. Richard crept across the lawn and threw a pebble up to call her, and then another, but got no response. He couldn't think of any other way of attracting her attention, short of breaking the window.

Richard retreated to the end of the garden. He sat in the moonlight on the cold stone wall rubbing out the lipstick mark on his cheek and wondered why he was the only one who'd actually been asked to leave.

The fracas at the dinner table put a severe limit on visitors. Too many people there interfered with Jay's painting. From now on, no outsiders would be allowed into the magic circle. This did not include Richard. Lucia said his presence was essential. Richard was flattered and the feelings of exclusion that he'd nursed out in the garden began to fade.

It was still very hot and Jay often chose to paint in the cooler evening time. Richard was often invited to stay on and eat with the family. He was helping Clio clear away one night, when Lucia came up behind him.

'Richard?' Her voice was rich and seductive. She seldom called him 'Ricardo' now, which was a relief, but he still jumped slightly when she called him 'Richard', faintly surprised to hear her speak his real name. 'Would you like your fortune read?'

'Of course he would,' Clio spoke for him. A habit she was developing when he was with the family. 'Wouldn't you?' she added as an afterthought.

'Yes, I guess,' he replied. 'I've never had it read before.'

'Come over here then.' Lucia beckoned him over to the table. 'What will it be?' she asked. 'Cards or crystal?'

'Go for the cards, mate,' Joe advised from the sofa. 'She never sees anything in the crystal ball.'

'Shut up, Joe,' Clio said. 'What do you know about it?'

'Never sees anything for me, anyway.' Joe took a good long toke on the joint he was smoking.

'That's because your future's obscured by clouds of weed smoke. If you've got one at all.'

'Crystal it is then.'

Lucia went to the cabinet where she kept various items to do with divination and magic: tarot cards wrapped in a yellow silk scarf, a thin forked hazel wand, a bundle of sticks for the I Ching, rune staves in a hand-woven bag. She carried the crystal ball, shrouded in black velvet, over to the table. She held it cradled, as if it were fragile and special,

159

like a rare bird's egg. She put it down gently in the centre of the table and set candles to burn on either side.

'Come over here, Richard. Sit opposite me.' Richard did as he was told. 'Now, have you any coin to give me? Preferably silver.'

'Will this do?' Richard rummaged about in his pocket and came up with a fifty-pence piece.

'Admirably.' She held out her hand. 'Now put it in my palm. That's it.'

She closed her hand over the coin, transferring it to a little worn velvet purse with a metal snap at the top. Only now did she unfold the velvet, lying this flat to act as a mat to the crystal ball. She passed her hand over the shining sphere and back again. The surface misted slightly from the heat of her palm. She made another few passes, this way, then that, as if she was warming it up in some way, then she gazed down into the depths.

'This is the bit when she starts to make it up.' Joe laughed. 'You could do the fairs, Lucia, I swear it.'

'Hush! I'm concentrating. Silence now from everybody. I need to focus.'

Silence grew, filling the space around them until even Joe's giggles subsided. The moon shone through the uncurtained window, adding a golden glow to the yellow candlelight. Noises seeped in from outside and then faded: an owl hooting, off at some distance, the drone of a farm vehicle returning home from a long day harvesting out in the sun-bleached fields. Nobody moved in the room. Everybody sat very still watching Lucia as she stared into the crystal. Richard could see nothing special, just the deep black of the cloth, a little barred patch where the windows were reflected, the candles' flicker. Nevertheless, he could see how it might work. Stare at the same place for a long

160

time and the effect is hypnotic, shapes began to stretch and slide . . .

Lucia began to speak, slowly at first, then with more authority. No one made any sound, each gaze locked on her. The low, musical voice held them with a strange mesmeric power.

'I see you. At least I think it's you. Down by the sea. Standing on the very edge of the shore. There are white shapes whirling all around you. Birds? Yes. They must be.' She paused, frowning as if the image was hard to fix and capture. 'It's gone.' She sighed her frustration. 'No. Wait.' She held up her hand as if to quell any potential disturbance. 'It's very cloudy, but I can see the whirling white shapes . . . It's not the same, though. The sea is very stormy. And you're wearing something quite extraordinary . . .' She paused again. 'That's it, I think. It's all gone over to black.'

She raised the corners of the black velvet cloth one at a time to cover the crystal.

'How strange!' She looked at Richard. 'You were wearing bright yellow trousers right up to your armpits!'

'Waders,' Richard supplied. 'I've got some I wear for fishing.'

'You saw Richard fishing!' Joe began giggling again. 'Did he catch anything? Get her to take another look, mate. See if you're using the right bait.'

Richard grinned and shifted in his seat. He'd had few expectations as to what Lucia might see. He'd quickly dismissed visions of himself on a stage with a rock band, or running out for the Villa at Wembley, but he was a bit disappointed. Fishing? It was bizarre and mundane at the same time. It made no more sense to him than it did to Joe.

161

Lucia gave her son a look designed to wither. 'He didn't have a rod or anything, not that I could see. Besides, that's not the point. Divination is not supposed to be precise. If there is meaning there, it will unfold.' She returned the crystal to the cabinet. 'I Ching. That's more exact. It might help interpret.'

'The one with the little sticks?' Joe groaned. 'That's even more boring and takes ages. Time to fold your gypsy tent, Lucia.'

Lucia gave her son another look. 'The I Ching is not just fortune telling! It is a serious way of putting the individual in touch with what is happening in his or her life, what possible courses of action to take. It is 5,000 years old. The Chinese treat it as practically their Bible—'

'Yeah, yeah.' Her son laughed. 'Whatever you say, Lucia.'

She ignored him. 'What do you think, Jay? You used to like the I Ching.'

'What?' Jay looked up from his chair. He had been sprawled there the whole time, eyes closed. Richard didn't even think he'd been listening. 'No. Enough for tonight. I agree with Joe.'

He closed his eyes again and went back to a place he could see in his mind where a boy stood alone on the shore with white birds flying all around him.

Clio signalled to Richard with her eyes. No one seemed to notice or care as they got up to leave. Richard followed her across the moonlit lawn. The full moon had changed from gold to silver, like a turning coin. He and Clio used its brightness to sneak off, escaping to the dark woods, or down to the pale dunes and the silky cold sand. There they would enter the private world that existed only when they were alone together. How many days? How many nights? He'd lost count and he did not want to think about it. He wanted only the wildness, the intimacy that still held him breathless, filled with a hunger that fed on itself, a longing that could never be satisfied.

Triptych: Right- and Left-hand Panels

Clio (1969–73)
Group of four paintings (two each side)
90.2 x 61 cm
oil on panel
Jethro Arnold Dalton R.A. (1916–1976)

Never shown during the artist's lifetime, this series of paintings is of Clio Dalton, the artist's daughter. Now owned by Charles Hammond, Dalton's astonishingly beautiful nude studies have picked up a great deal of notoriety since the artist's untimely demise. Whatever claims have been made about the portraits and how Hammond came by them, these paintings remain truly exquisite and they should be judged for their artistic quality alone.

(M. H. Randolf, *Sunday Times*, 25 May 1980)

'Every exploration is valid. For me, the sacred is contained within the profane.' J.A.D., 1968

No matter how warm the day before, or how hot it would become, the mornings had a coolness about them, with damp drifting in from the sea and mist rising from the valleys like the first breath of autumn. Soon he would be leaving. Holiday over. Nothing lasts forever. The thoughts stole across his consciousness as he walked up to the Wish House each day, playing there like the refrain of a song he couldn't get out of his head. They both knew. It was in her kiss. The way she held him. It lent an extra sweetness to each meeting, but the words remained unspoken. To say them would make it real.

Jay was the only one who knew how little time there was left. He had to finish the painting, so Richard had to tell him. It was only fair.

'That's all right.' The painter grinned at him. 'Not much more to do now. Better get on with it, then. Now, where was I?'

He went back to his work. He had reversed the sittings, so Richard came to him in the morning. Something to do with the light, he'd said, and now time was short he wanted to concentrate on Richard. He looked tired, his face more drawn than when Richard had first met him, his eyes seemed deeper set, with dark rings under them. His head shook, ever so slightly, as he stared at the canvas. He took up a long stick, lodging its padded end against the edge of the canvas, resting his wrist to hold the brush steady as he added fine detail to the almost finished painting.

'What's that thing called?' Richard asked.

'It's called a maulstick.'

'You haven't used it before,' Richard remarked

The artist didn't answer. Somewhere below the phone was ringing and ringing. Jay ignored it. He never answered it anyway, even if he wasn't working. The ringing stopped.

'Jay?' Lucia called up the stairs.

When he didn't reply, she came to deliver the message herself.

'It's Charles,' she said, calling up from under the trap-door.

'What does he want?'

'To see you.'

'Tell him he can't. I've got work to do. I thought I said no more people.'

'Too late. He's calling from the village. He's taken a room. He's on his way up here.'

'Christ! I thought she meant he was on the phone from London.' Jay wiped his hands on a rag. 'That's all I need.'

He left the room without a word. Richard followed their voices downstairs until what they were saying was too indistinct to make out. He had been concentrating so hard that he was still standing in position. He gradually unfroze and stepped out from his pose. It was like being a human statue. All he ever did in this room was come in and stand still. It felt odd to be moving about wearing these clothes, as though he was walking around inside the picture.

He had not been able to view the painting before. He went over to have a look. He frowned. It made him look bigger, fleshier, younger than he felt. It was not unflattering. Not exactly. It was more that the picture exposed aspects of himself, an awkward, gauche quality that he would rather people didn't see. That's what *he* saw anyway. He turned from the painting with a sigh of disappointment.

He looked around. Before, he'd only been able to explore the room with his eyes from a fixed point. Now he could move about. Sometimes Jay slept in here when he worked at night and didn't want to disturb Lucia. A narrow iron-framed single bed stood against the far wall. It was covered in a heap of grey-brown hairy army blankets. Next to it was a packing case, a stub of candle on it. That was all. It was as austere as a monk's cell, or an army barracks. There was an old canvas case under the bed, its re-enforced corner poking out, like some animal's snout. Richard pushed at it with his foot. He was tempted to squat down and take a look at some of the papers that prevented the lid from shutting, but they might all come spilling out and he might not be able to get them back in again.

He stood up and went over to the racks which took up one whole wall. This was where Jay kept the paintings he had not sold and did not want displayed. Richard pulled a few out at random. Seascapes, and more seascapes. They all looked the same, or very similar. Although Richard could see that there were differences in light and weather, the state of the tide and the sea itself, they did not interest him particularly. He stepped back, vaguely disappointed. These paintings were so boring. He'd spent weeks staring at these enigmatic racks, wondering what was so special, what it was that Jay wanted kept so private. Curiosity had overcome any guilt he might be feeling; nevertheless he jumped when he heard the back door open then close. Voices drifted up from below him. He'd better get a move on if he was going to check out the rest of the paintings. He wouldn't get this kind of chance again.

He worked his way further along, inhaling the linseed scent of the oil paint that seemed to exude from the canvases, intensified by the warmth of the air in the room. It

169

was a smell that would become imprinted, so that ever afterwards, just one whiff of it would bring him back here.

Clio 9, Clio 10, Clio 11, Clio 12 scrawled in thick black pencil on the narrow smudged edge of nailed white canvas. Richard pulled them out one at a time.

Clio painted in a series of luminous spaces. In each of the pictures she was naked, but the images were robbed of any context, so the nude figures seemed to be floating in a nebulous world outside reality. The first one he pulled out had a fiery intensity, the pale figure bathed in orange-red light. The next was entirely golden, her hair and skin gilded as if lit by a waning, autumn sun. Another was entirely blue, with a cold infinity with the child frozen in the centre like a beautiful cadaver. The last was all shades of green, tinging even the skin, making the creature within elfin. Other-worldly. But the images were real. All too real. And beautiful.

Such beauty was hard to look at. Richard had to shift his gaze away and to the side, as if caught by a light too bright, or by a being of such absolute beauty that to look straight at it would blind. The artist had caught her at the points of transition, from childhood to girlhood and girl to adolescent. No coyness. Rather the opposite. There was absolute honesty coupled with a ravishing intensity; a challenging innocence that was not innocent at all. Richard had seen that look before. For him, the paintings were supercharged with the power of *her*. The power she had over him. A power that reverberated through him like a hollow booming that threatened to go on and on and never stop until it broke him apart. Richard had seen enough. He pushed the paintings back one by one. The last caught on a nail. There was the sharp, loud ripping sound of stiff fabric tearing under pressure. Richard pushed harder. The tearing

170

got worse, but Richard didn't care. The destruction gave him satisfaction, it salved the raw place that the paintings had opened up within him like an application of soothing balm.

He went to the window and stared out, seeing but not seeing Jay and Hammond arguing below him in the garden. All he felt for her, all he could ever feel for her, was nothing. It could never match the love shown here. But what kind of love was it? What kind of love could have painted that?

'That's the back of him.' Jay came in rubbing his hands together. 'Better not see him round here again. I called him a friend once. He's turned into a shark just like the rest of them. I don't know why they don't bottle our blood and sell it. Maybe one day they will, and we won't have to bother with any of this painting lark. Calls himself a Cultural Commentator now! What does that mean? Pretentious bastard!' Jay gave a harsh, humourless laugh and fixed Richard with his brooding stare. 'What's the matter with you? You've got a face like a smacked arse.'

Richard shook his head. 'Nothing.'

'OK, then. Get back in position.'

'I've got to . . .' Richard began to say. He desperately wanted to leave. Go now. Straight away. He was sorry he hadn't taken the chance to get away while he still could.

'Got to what?'

'Go.'

'No.' Jay looked at him with flat black eyes. 'I need you here. You're not going anywhere. There's still work to do.'

Richard looked away. He didn't feel strong enough to defy him. He would have to do as he was told.

Jay studied him for a little while, Richard staring straight ahead. Then he looked away from his subject, his eyes searched the room, taking it in section by section. Richard began to sweat inside his clothes. He did not follow the artist's gaze, knowing that he was bound to see it, his eye trained to notice every little changing detail, no matter how slight.

He went over to the racks, giving a little grunt as if what he saw confirmed something. Richard risked a panicky look sideways and saw the long fingers splayed out, pushing at the painting that stuck out ever so slightly. There was a faint ripping sound as the canvas caught on the unseen nail, or whatever it was. The artist gave another grunt, of annoyance and frustration this time.

'Now, what's happened here?' He rocked the painting gently backwards and forwards, trying to work it loose. Then he glanced over at Richard, who managed to look away just in time.

'That's it!' He left the snagged canvas and returned to his easel. 'That's the look you had when I first saw you. I've been waiting to see that again.'

He dabbled a fine brush in different pools of pigment and began to paint.

He said nothing for a while. Richard did not lose his nervousness, neither did he relax. He felt trapped in the silence between them. Unable to leave, frozen in place like a statue, he began to dread what the artist would say to him if he did speak.

'Tell me, Richard –' The deep voice made him jump. The artist smiled with what could have been satisfaction, but the words he spoke next were not what Richard expected. '– do you have things that you don't want to share? Things that you don't want other people to see?'

Richard nodded his head slightly. Didn't everybody?

'That's what this is all about. That's what Hammond

172

wants off me,' Jay went on, his mind jumping back to the argument in the garden. It was as if he was talking to himself. 'Paintings are like confessionals. Ever kept a diary, have you?' Richard nodded. 'Embarrassing, isn't it?' He laughed, a sharp harsh bark. 'Getting older only makes it worse. All those younger selves crowding round to haunt and mock, laughing at how old you've got.' He paused to think. 'Are you Catholic?'

Richard shook his head again and winced at the shooting pain in the back of his neck. All the tension, added to the way he had to stand, was giving him a headache.

'I'm not, either. Don't believe in anything, in fact, but I've always envied them. Confession sounds like a good thing to me. A way to keep your sanity. And we all need that. Good for the soul, isn't that what they say? Do you have things to confess, Richard? Things you feel guilty about?'

Richard gave a slight shrug of the shoulders as they paraded past him: everything from the way he'd been neglecting his parents and Dylan to how he'd ripped that painting just now. For once, he was glad that he was not encouraged to talk.

'I bet you do,' the artist answered for him. 'And they'll get worse as you get older. Fester away inside you, in secret.'

He stopped speaking, the silence returning.

'I don't trust psychotherapy,' he continued after a time. 'Load of claptrap. But that's how painting works for me. That's why they aren't all for everybody to see. Not everyone shares my way of seeing. People could misunderstand. Misinterpret. I've told Hammond that he cannot have them. He'll have to wait until after I'm dead.'

Richard's eyes slid to the racks on the wall. He thought he knew which paintings Hammond wanted.

'Stop fidgeting about!' The artist scowled at his movement. 'How many times do I have to tell you! I will not accept anything less than perfection. In this endeavour, we are captured both together. The painter and the painted. You remember that.'

Richard never forgot.

They finished the session in silence, Richard's headache growing. By the time Jay let him go, it felt like someone was drilling into the base of his skull.

'What's up?' Clio asked as he came downstairs. 'You don't look so good.'

'I don't feel so good – I've got a thumping headache.'

'What's good for that?' Clio frowned. She really was hopeless without Lucia around.

'Aspirin?' Richard suggested. 'Paracetamol?'

'No.' Clio looked shocked. 'They're *bad* for you. Aspirin makes your stomach bleed. Paracetamol attacks the liver. No, I was thinking more of remedies, but Lucia's gone out collecting . . .'

'Collecting what?'

More ingredients for remedies, no doubt. Lucia was a great one for alternative medicines, but the pain in his head was so bad he could hardly keep his eyes focused. It wasn't going to respond to powdered bat's wing, or tea made with anything. The only thing to shift it would be a couple of his mother's Vegenin.

'She's looking for mushrooms. It was damp this morning.'

'Why doesn't she just buy some?'

'Because you can't buy the kind she's collecting,' Clio said, as if she was explaining to an idiot. 'Not in this country.'

Richard closed his eyes and squeezed the bridge of his

nose. Sometimes he lost patience. All the money they've
got, and she was always coming back with baskets full of
odd stuff. 'Food for free', they called it. Richard stole a
look out of the window at the Witches' Garden.

'She'll poison the lot of you, if you're not careful.'

Clio laughed. 'She knows what she's doing. She's check-
ing for late cherries, early plums and blackberries. She
wants to make some jam. Your friend Dylan's helping her.
He says he knows some places.'

'I bet he does.'

So Dylan was continuing his campaign of 'botanical
seduction'. Despite the pain in his head, Richard almost
smiled.

Clio wanted him to stay until after her session with Jay
was over, but his headache was nowhere near going and he
wanted an excuse to get away. He wanted to ask her about
the pictures he'd seen. What did they mean? But he wasn't
sure he dared do that. He'd be better off going back to the
caravan. It would give him a chance to think it all out.

Chronicles #2
'Lad & Girl Love'

(1976) Ink on cartridge paper
21 x 29.7 cm
Jethro Arnold Dalton R.A. (1916–1976)

One of the few surviving of a series of extraordinary drawings made just before the artist's death. The subject matter is clearly erotic, but the figures are almost abstract, all individuality lost in the fluidity of form. The quick, deft, effortless line is almost Oriental, but with an iconic solidity that is very like sculpture. Only recently released from the artist's estate, these drawings have been described as 'among the very greatest expressions of erotic art; a celebration of human love that is universal.'

(E. Baines, *Art in Focus*, 1980)

If anyone had been home, if he'd had his key with him, he might never have gone back again, never have seen what he did, and everything that happened afterwards might never have happened.

By the time he got back to the Wish House it was past two o'clock. Clio would be well into her session by now. He knocked lightly, thinking Lucia would be back. When he got no answer, he pushed at the door. It was locked. Which was odd. They never locked the door unless everybody had gone out. He'd thought Jay and Clio would be in working, but they must have gone off somewhere. He had not expected that. Richard looked around, discomfited and disappointed. His head was still paining him and the light was blinding; he wanted to get out of it more than anything. There was a stillness all around him. His damp skin was flecked with little black insects and there was a humid heaviness in the air, as though a thunderstorm was forming, although there wasn't a cloud. The sun shone pitiless and white from a sky like polished pewter. He squinted up at the house, cursing. He was seeing in splinters. He'd left his sunglasses in the 'van that morning. He could certainly do with them now. Then he remembered something. Lucia kept a spare key under one of the geranium pots. She never carried keys with her and had put it there for those occasions, like this, when the ever open door was locked.

He moved the sun-warmed terracotta, breathing in the sharp pungency of the plants. The flowers were falling;

petals sprayed across his hands like bright red drops of arterial blood. Richard shut his eyes and opened them. All his senses seemed heightened. Maybe it was his headache. Random thoughts and observations came and went, mixed with flashes of memory: these pots on the first day, Lucia on the sun-crisped lawn, how the grass looked blue in the moonlight, looking up at Clio's window, the curtains drawn.

He took the key and let himself into the cool darkness of the house. He sighed. It was a relief after being outside. He staggered, almost blind, over to the sofa and threw himself down, his arm over his eyes. He'd just rest there, maybe sleep for a bit; that sometimes cured the headache without him having to take anything for it. He worried it could be the migraine that sent his mother to her room to lie in the dark for hours with a wet flannel on her forehead.

The thoughts frothing on the surface of his mind began to subside and gradually the pain began to ebb, bit by little bit. The house was very quiet now. You could hear every sound. The faint clink of a near motionless wind chime from outside, the washing machine churning, clicking through its cycles . . .

Richard's drifting attention was caught by a low murmur coming from the floor above. He opened his eyes. There were people up there. He must have been sleeping. How else could they have got past him and up the stairs? Either that, or they had been here the entire time.

Richard looked at his watch. He knew Jay didn't like being disturbed while he was painting, but they should be finishing soon. He stood up and went to the stairs. He'd just go to the studio and pop his head through the trapdoor, let them know he was here.

The studio was empty. Richard stepped back down the

ladder. The session must have been cancelled or cut short, which was most unusual. Jay was a stickler for routines as far as work was concerned. Could set a watch by him, that's if any of them had one. They must have gone out after all.

Richard frowned and listened. Perhaps he'd been hearing things, or maybe someone had left the radio on. No, there it was again, a low murmuring. Intimate. Two voices, one female. It sounded like Clio. The other voice was too low to identify but the laugh was definitely male. The sound was coming from Clio's room. Richard edged nearer to the door. There was water on the floor, as though she'd just had a shower.

Who could be in there with her? It had to be Dylan. He'd always been after Clio really, not Lucia. It was so obvious now. Richard trod silently, determined to catch them together. Dylan might be bigger, but Richard had surprise on his side. He'd punch his head in for this. Richard's fists curled and uncurled at his side. He would kill him.

The door was old, made of planks which were warped in places. The thick, pungent, familiar scent of marijuana curled through the cracks. Richard peered through one of the spaces. What he saw made him pull back fast, as if his own eye had been met by another looking back.

Clio was lying on the bed, naked except for a towel half draped over her legs. She drew on a joint, a quick, sharp intake of breath, and held it up to a figure half turned away from her, silhouetted against the window. The light diffused through the drawn curtains made the room red inside, like a crimson cave. The man was tall, long haired, dark skinned, skinny and unmistakably naked. A sinewy arm reached out as he leaned down to take the joint from her, his face obscured by his falling hair.

It was Jay. Richard knew straight away. He tore himself

from the gap in the door and stood with his back against the wall, blinking as if to clear his vision. His whole body was shaking, his breath coming so shallow and fast that he felt he might faint. He put his hands on his knees to steady himself, sucking in deep draughts of air. His mind was empty of any thought and, with his eyes closed or open, all he could see was the two of them together. The shock of what he'd seen had burned itself instantly on to his mind and memory, so that it would always be there, for the rest of his life, ready to come back to him, at odd times of the day, in dreams and on waking, always as vivid as a moment ago.

He wasn't aware of any conscious decision, but his feet took him up to Jay's studio. He didn't care that he wasn't supposed to be there; he cared even less that they might find him, not that it seemed very likely, seeing that they were otherwise occupied.

He sniffed as he entered the room. It smelt faintly of the sea and iodine, a subtle reek of marine decay coming from the desiccating lengths of bladderwrack hanging from the window sill. Inside, instead of out. That meant something.

The gown Clio had been wearing was hanging from a beam. The material swished and swung on its hook as he went past it, glittery and thin, brushing his bare arm as he dropped the trap, feeling slippery as her hair, cold as a fish's skin.

He looked about him at the easel and canvases, the squeezed and mangled tubes, the table Jay used as a palette, the fresh squirms from the day's sessions congealing into blackening clots. He picked up a thin-bladed palette knife, testing the blade with his thumb until he saw a beaded line of bright blood. Sharp enough to cut. He held it by the wooden handle, gripped like a dagger. The canvas on the easel. Clio as a mermaid. Richard moved nearer. You could never tell with Jay, but the painting looked finished. That would be even better. His fingers tightened round the knife.

He glanced over to the racks that held the other canvases. The ones of Clio as a child. His eyes slid towards them as his mind had been sliding back to them ever since this morning. Everywhere he looked, what he saw gathered new meaning. Everything was suddenly clear.

Richard went over to the racks on the wall. He stepped boldly where before he had walked on tiptoe. He no longer cared if he was found up here.

A portfolio had been taken out and was leaning against the racks. It was covered in swirly pink and grey-green marbling, like the endpapers of old books. The corners were worn, bent over, yellowy cardboard showing through. The red ribbon that secured the top had faded to rose. As Richard went to move it, the cover fell open and hit the floor with a dull thud. Papers flew up and scattered, disarranged by the sudden draught of air. They settled back in an untidy heap. Richard bent down to gather them together. Then his hand froze.

He flushed red, the blood beating in his head, thudding in his ears, even though there was no one else to witness. Pages torn from a sketch pad, graphic drawings in the style of book illustrations; scribbled notes underneath identified them as scenes from *The Chronicles of Pryderi*. Richard picked up one, then another. There could be nothing like this in the published book. He stared, transfixed. Blood from his thumb smeared and dripped as the paper shook and bent in his tightening grip. He felt numb, paralysed, his brain refusing to order the implications of what he was seeing. To be betrayed to such a degree did not seem possible. He did not see any beauty there, although the pen and ink drawing was perfect, the line exquisite. He was blind to the essential innocence of the images. All he saw was Clio's face, and his own nakedness. He felt violated. The moments shown here were absolutely personal, intensely private. Not to be shared with anyone. First time. First love. They were to be kept in his memory, each one pristine. To be carried through a lifetime. And here they were ruined, besmirched and sullied forever. His hands were shaking with anger as he searched through the papers in front of him.

He slammed the covers together, shutting the images in the portfolio, tightly knotting the strings. He looked up at the racks of paintings above him. His first impulse when he came in here had been to go berserk, turn the place over, slash and smash, crush and trample, but there were better things to do than that.

Triptych: Central Panel

Clio 1978 (ME)

180 x 180 cm

Oil on panel

Final Show

Clio Dalton (1960–)

Central Panel

Although the figure is clothed, the work is arresting in its naked rawness. It is as though many layers have been stripped away from the Dalton paintings shown on the opposing panels where the shadowy child seems to have been robbed of her humanity, idealized, veiled in her nakedness, transformed into some sort of fey child–woman fetish.

Clio Dalton allows very little resemblance, although she was the model for those paintings and this is a self-portrait. This child is real. The head is pulled back, the mouth open, teeth bared, a black hole in the face. The painting has none of the grace, the smooth, suave, seductive pale bisque perfection of Dalton's meticulous child figures. The body is painted in awkward and angular strokes, the fists are bundles of aggressive rage. The thick application of paint suggests hair that is wet, plastered to the head. The face is streaked with red: raw flesh, leaking emotion. The limbs are similarly splashed with pigment: muddy, besmirched, providing yet another element of realism and ironic comment . . .

(Examiner's comments)

Richard had set off a train of events and he couldn't care less about which way they went, he did not stop to think that he might be caught in the consequences. He went back to the caravan site via the village. He left the parcel of paintings at the inn, *for the attention of Charles Hammond.*

Then he disposed of the portfolio, bending and breaking the cardboard carrier, tearing the pictures into tiny bits, dumping the lot in the big battered bins behind the toilet block. He hung around long enough to see some woman deposit her plastic bucketful of tea leaves and peelings on top. After that, he went fishing with his dad.

They came back early. Almost as soon as they got down to the rocks, the wind started getting up, whipping the lines about. They set up, but the swell was growing with the incoming tide, sending biggish waves over their feet. Seawater slopped into the tackle and bait boxes, forcing them to retreat. Out at sea, the storm that had threatened all day was building, the cloud piling up in great towers of purple and grey. When the sun went in, the temperature began to plummet. They were in shorts and sandals and could look forward to a soaking. It was time to call it a day.

Richard had not been back long when there was a sharp knock on the caravan door, followed by another.

'Get that, Richard, will you?'

Richard didn't move. It had to be Clio, but what would he say? All afternoon he'd been going over what he'd done. He could justify it to himself, he had no problem with that, but she would *never* understand. Not unless he explained, and he didn't want to do that. It would be better if he never saw her again, but she knew where he was and was bound to come after him. The things that he'd seen came into his head again. How could he talk about that to her?

His mother sighed when he didn't get up and marked her page by turning down the corner. She squinted at her son through the smoke of her cigarette, but he pretended that he hadn't heard and wouldn't look at her. She put her book aside with a further exaggerated sigh and went slowly to the door.

'There's a girl.' His mother turned. 'Wants to see you.'

Richard went down the steps, forcing Clio to step back, closing the door behind him.

She didn't waste time.

'Why did you do it?'

'Why did I do what?'

He didn't want his mother hearing any of this. He began walking away from the van, forcing her to follow him if she wanted to go on talking.

'You know. It was you, wasn't it?'

Richard shrugged and walked on. There was no good place to have a row on a caravan site, but they were not the campers' main focus of attention. The wind was blowing harder now and rain was falling in fat spots. The air smelt of scorched dust. People were rushing round taking in washing, packing up canvas chairs, padded loungers, picnic tables, anything that might get wet or blown about. Richard hoped that they were all going to be kept too busy to notice him and Clio.

'What did you think you'd get? Money? How much did you think the paintings you stole were worth?'

The scouring contempt in her voice made Richard turn round.

'I didn't think anything like that. I didn't ask him for anything. I just left them inside the door. How did you know it was me?'

'Had to be, didn't it? Anyway, Hammond said it was – when he bought them back. The woman in the pub described you. How did you think he could keep them? Or would want to? It's *stealing*, for one thing.' She shook her head. 'You know nothing. You are so stupid!

'Why did you do it? How *could* you?' she went on, not giving him any time to answer. 'After Jay's been so good to you. And Lucia. Even Joe. I thought you liked us. You'd become part of the family. And what about me? I thought –' Her eyes narrowed. 'You're a snake in the grass, you know that? A real little snake in the grass.'

He waited until the storm of words was over.

'I didn't want to hurt *you*,' he started to say.

'Oh, that's good! Of course you hurt me! Anything that hurts Jay is bound to hurt me!'

'I saw you,' he said. 'This afternoon. It's . . . it's not right, Clio,' he went on in a rush to stop her interrupting, knowing he would only be able to say this once. 'I know you probably can't say no, and it has to be very difficult. But . . . but . . .' He paused. If anything, the looks she was giving him were even wilder. This was hard to talk about. Almost impossible. But he made himself go on. 'I thought . . . I thought that if other people knew, or if *he* thought they might find out . . . it would make him stop, stop doing that to you.'

'What are you talking about?'

'The pictures,' he went on quickly, determined that she should hear him out. 'The ones he painted when you were a kid. And the drawings. Of you and me. It's like . . .' He was finally running out of words to say. 'It's like nothing is

189

sacred. And maybe it isn't to him. Not in the same way as everybody else. All that stuff about Druids and sacred groves and being a pagan. He is exceptional,' he added, anticipating what he thought might be one of her arguments. 'I know that. He has an exceptional talent, but in every other way, he's just a man. The same rules apply to him, the same as everybody else.'

She did not reply at first. She was shaking, having difficulty keeping control.

'You think it was Jay!' She said it quietly, almost unbelieving, but hysteria was rising within her, bubbling in her throat, until it seemed that she might choke. 'That's why you did it, isn't it? You think I was with Jay. Oh, my God!'

She began to laugh. A tinny high-pitched giggle that started in her nose and then erupted, gurgling up from down deep inside her, spewing forth in a series of hooting caterwauls before settling into a rhythm of rocking guffaws that Richard thought would never stop. She held her arms folded tightly round her, as if she was trying to hold herself together. She was shaking her head, her wet hair flailing, as thin as whips. She laughed until she was sobbing and gasping, mouth wedged open, tears seeping from eyes screwed tight shut. This was clearly hysteria. Richard's hand itched and twitched, he wanted to hit her, slap her, but he kept his fist bunched in his pocket. He just had to stand by, waiting for the gale to subside. People were openly staring, outdoor furniture forgotten. If they weren't getting looks before, they were now.

'It wasn't Jay, you idiot!' she gasped when she finally stopped. 'How could you have even thought that! That is sick!'

Richard couldn't look at her. Fear that he might have been mistaken turned his eyes away. He must have misunderstood something. Shame began to spread over him like dozens of hot needles pricking at his skin. The heat seemed to seep back into him, flowing down along his very bones.

'OK. So, who . . . who was it, then?' he had to ask eventually. 'You were with somebody.'

She didn't answer straight away, wanting his embarrassment, his humiliation, to go on as long as possible.

'It was Hammond. If you must know. Not that it's your business. You could have saved yourself the trouble if you'd only known. Just delivered the paintings straight to my room!'

He thought she was going to start laughing again and stepped back as if from the threat of a physical blow.

'For how long?' he asked. He didn't want to speak to her, but he had to know.

'A while. But why should I tell you about it?' Her gaze slid from Richard to the neat rows of caravans, the parked cars: Rovers, Marinas and Cortinas. 'You are far too ordinary to understand.'

He'd made a mistake about Jay. She had a right to be angry about that and he was sorry. But Hammond? That had come out of nowhere. Richard had been going to apologize, but now he didn't want to. Hammond was old. He could be her father. To Richard, that was nearly as bad.

She turned on him. 'Haven't you got *anything* to say?'

He shook his head.

'That's it, then,' she said, anger and sarcasm ebbing out of her. She shivered, as though suddenly aware that it was raining, that she was getting soaked. 'I'm not going to see you again. None of us are. So what does it matter what you think?'

With that, she marched off, her arms folded tightly

round herself, her hair hanging down in swinging strings, her head bent against the driving rain. That was the last he saw of her, striding through the puddles, the red mud splashing all up her bare legs.

seascape #452

(1976) Oil on paper

Estate of the artist

J. A. Dalton R.A. (1916–1976)

Dark sea, long diagonals, battleship grey to charcoal, bottle-glass green in the waves curling to shore. Sun - pale gleam off to the left, saffron/sulphur obliquely illuminating breaking waves white/yellow, steel gleam here and there, troughs in black/blue shadow. Sky - dark grey nimbus, muscular, bunching like fists, slanting rain smudging horizon. Mackerel pattern streaming to zenith. White birds wheeling. Distant headland to left: black-green smudge, obscured by mist.

Artist's notes: Sketchbook #50

Dalton painted the same spot on the coast just below his house, meticulously recording every change in tide and weather.

'Why should I not? The view is new. Fresh each day. The challenge is constant. The possibilities are infinite. The sea goes on forever.'

('J. A. Dalton: Last Conversations', Charles Hammond – *New Arts Review*, December 1976)

He had been studying the same spot, from the same angle, the same exact gap between the earth and the sky for many years now. He'd painted this view from the beach more times than he could remember, at every state of the tide, every point of the year, but he knew that this would be the very last time.

'*There* lies the beauty! *There* lies the wonder,' he whispered, although there was no one to hear him as he loaded his brush with paint. The tremor in his hands was worse now, much worse than it had been before. He was alone on the long beach, except for a pair of fishermen, far enough away not to matter, casting into the crashing surf. They were both dressed in foul-weather gear, chrome-yellow chest-high waders. Miniaturized by distance, they stood like models set at exactly the same angle, the smaller one slightly forward from the other, the long sea-angling rods slim as toothpicks in their hands. He held his elbow braced as a spasm shook his body. The cramps were getting stronger. He closed his fist against the grip and twist in his guts and bent over further. His long dark hair swung out, touching his palette, picking up tiny blobs of white and yellow from the surface. A cold sweat broke out over his face, beading across his forehead. He bit his lip, partly against the pain, but also testing for the numbness that was set to follow. If he was going to do it, he'd better get on with it. No telling how long he could carry on.

Still he did not get started, did not touch the brush on to the white surface. He stared at the cold breakers, at the brown churning sand and pebbles, at the white-topped waves, at the distant headland obscured by mist and spray, at the rain like iron filings slanting to the horizon, at the horizon itself, curving between heaven and earth. The vanishing point.

He gazed, but his eye was turning inwards, the view was becoming obscured, overlaid by memory. A faculty he distrusted as a painter, even more as a man.

Lycidas

(1976) Oil on canvas
204.5 x 257.2cm
John. A. Dalton
(1869–1948)

Valued more as a patron of others than as an artist in his own right, this is his last, and without doubt most successful, example of his work. Dalton's insistence on painting in a deeply unfashionable classical style certainly didn't help his dream of becoming a respected painter. Add a certain lack of fluidity, a woodenness of execution, and it is easy to see why the acclaim he craved eluded him. Apart from this one painting. His last. Approaching death, or the poignant nature of the subject matter, perhaps allowed him to reach . . .

(Exhibition notes, *Whitehall Galleries*, 1958)

The sea has gone, leaving only a wide expanse of sand. The sky is blue, the sun is golden. The distant strip of water shines like a wedding band. A figure is running towards it, further, and still further. He disturbs the flocks of seabirds that wander the exposed foreshore. They whirl up in a flurry as he races through them. They circle around him as he stands still now, right at the edge of the sea; a scatter of white flecks turning to silver as their wings catch the sun. His shape becomes indistinct, shimmering in and out of the halo of light that distance has formed around it. The boy on the shore waits and watches. The blood running from his nose goes sticky, then dries to a hard lacquer, pulling his skin tight, holding his face as still as a mask.

After a time, he follows his brother down to the dangerous edge of the water, where the channel runs deep, churned by conflicting river currents that ruffle the surface into shining ridges and herringbone ripples. His brother is a strong swimmer and has come here where the water is deeper, but he has misjudged the tides, the state of the river. He has been taken and whirled away, helpless as a leaf, a piece of floating twig, and is nowhere to be seen. Then Jethro sees a waving arm, far, far out, and hears a shout, pitched high, a thin cry, too distant for the words to be distinct. The gesture says:

'Help! Help!'

Jethro hears his brother's shout loud inside his head. He looks up and down the beach. It is empty. There is no one to help. Out at sea, the arm is weakening, the head, bobbing like a seal, barely visible. Jethro has to squint hard to see it at all in between the restless rise and fall of the waves. Jethro almost turns away, but thinks that maybe someone else is seeing, someone else is watching. Maybe Father through the big brass telescope in his studio. Maybe God. Jethro doesn't want to, but this thought makes him enter the water. He takes one step, then another.

The sea is cold and the current is strong, even this near the shore. The sea is dangerous here. It is a dangerous shore. Goodness knows how many ships have been wrecked. They've been told the stories since early childhood. Told again, and again: 'The sea is dangerous here. It is a dangerous shore.' Bathers, fishermen, swept away by currents, pulled down by quicksand, cut off by the tides, by the branching, winding river. He feels the water tugging at his ankles, sucking the mud and small stones out from under his toes, so hard he nearly tumbles. He is a poor swimmer and does not like the water. He wades further. The swift current hits him in the back of the knees. His legs buckle as if he'd been kicked. If he falls he will be swept straight out to sea. What was the point in both of them drowning? He can't even see him any more. He turns back to the shore, his whole body pitched forward as he fights the strength of the current. The water parts and then rejoins itself, setting up little rilling waves around his calves. He's nearly there, nearly safe.

He turns back then to look again for his brother.

There is no sign of him. It is as though he has never been.

He runs up the beach, turning his back on the empty sea. The next thing he must do is find someone, tell someone. He can see himself running, see himself pointing, the men's heads bobbing up and down, like questing dogs, trying to see over the waves.

'Where, boy? Where exactly?'

He thinks he has the right place, but can't be sure. The light is beginning to fade and the tide is coming, faster than a train, racing over the sand, eating up the shore, making everything look different. Even while they stand looking out, it is lapping all around them, tugging at their feet, forcing them back.

Boats are launched, a search is started.

Jethro stays down on the shore.

'I'm waiting for my brother. Waiting for Richard,' he tells himself.

It is night-time before they find him. Dark. Lamps swing out, making shaky paths across the black water like the lamps used by the night-netting fishermen. There is one shout, then another; rocking and splashing as something heavy is hauled out of the water into the little craft. A motor comes sputtering to life. The two-stroke engine chugs laboriously to shore, the boat cutting a creamy arc through the water. A man stands in the bows, one foot up, leaning forward like a diver, ready to leap as soon as they reach the shallows.

The boy is there to see his brother brought ashore.

His lips are a pale cyan blue. His eyes, not quite closed, show like chips of cobalt from under long-spiked lashes. His skin gleams a pearly violet in the golden lamps; his wet hair lies coiled on his skull like curls carved in marble. He looks like a drowned angel. There is nothing anyone can do. The shouts of alarm and cries of horror become more muted, subsiding to sobs and tears. The boy stands by quietly, his eyes acting like a camera. He has that ability, even then. While he looks, his brain notes the unusual colours, the quality of the light, the exact disposition of the body: the angle of the head on the sand, the curve of the back, the crook of the knees as if he is running, the curl of the hand. His own fingers flex and cramp as if around a pencil or brush.

He feels a heavy hand on his shoulder, a rough finger brush the tears from his cheek.

'It's not your fault, son. You did what you could.'

The fisherman gives him a handkerchief to blow on. It is crumpled and stiff with salt.

Accidental death. That was the verdict. He went to the hearing wearing a new blue suit and a shirt and tie. He sat between his father and mother, going over his story, pulling at his collar that seemed to be strangling him, worrying about what he'd say. He'd been the last one to see him alive, but in the end nobody called him. No one ever asked him about anything. No one cared what he knew.

It nearly killed the old man. He was never the same after that. He'd go off to his studio at the same time every day just as he'd always done. It went on for years. Everyone in the house would pretend he was working, but he never painted another thing. No one knew what he did in there all day because nobody dared go in and find out. To disturb him would destroy the illusion. In the end, it was up to Jay. He came back from the war and couldn't stand it any more. Couldn't stand the pretence that the old man was painting. He had Parkinson's by then. His hands shaking so hard that he couldn't even hold a brush. Jay looked at his own hands' palsied movement. That was a twist he had never expected, even though he knew the disease could run in families. He no longer seemed able to control his face. His grin of recognition warped into a grimace.

He went in one day and found the old man staring out towards the sea through that big brass telescope. Behind him was a canvas blocked for a great big classical thing. It was based on Lycidas, the drowned youth. The old man had scrawled some Milton in a shaky hand across the bottom of the canvas:

> *For Lycidas is dead, dead ere his prime*
> *Young Lycidas, and hath not left his peer:*
> *who would not sing for Lycidas?*

Jay finished the painting for the old man. He let his brush sing for him.

He gave him a huge, wide, flaring, blue-black bruise of a sky, with a sickly streak of orange and saffron along the horizon, like he remembered it from that day. Just enough light to illuminate the body on the beach, gleaming on the pale marble flesh, shading the hollows in the greenish tones of death. He added classical bits, billowing drapery, filmy flicks of wispy material to hide the boy's nakedness. He put in some other figures. The faces he remembered lived again in the fishermen, the shepherds attracted down to the shore by the carry-on. He did it all in the old-master style that his father had so admired all his life, had tried so hard to copy and had failed so resoundingly to emulate – until now.

It was the only one of the old man's daubs to ever get anything like acclaim. It had toured to America in a big 'Pre-Raphaelites and Their Followers' exhibition and had been bought by a big foundation there. Jay never said a word about his own contribution. Anyway, the old man had been so gaga by then that he really believed that he'd done it himself. Jay hadn't wanted to disillusion him.

The painting was somewhere in America now. Jay

looked up. The sky had the exact same cast. He dabbed at his palette, loading his brush. Funny how things turn out.

Richard had not slept well. Usually, he liked the sound of rain on the caravan, but the insistent drumming and constant buffeting had kept him awake most of the night. He'd just get to sleep and the wind would thump against the side of the van, jolting him awake again. Once, he thought he heard sirens, but decided it must have been part of a dream or the screaming of the wind.

By morning, the storm had receded, the wind died almost to nothing, but it would have got the surf up and the tide was right. His father roused him at not much past first light to come down to the beach with him to take one last cast for bass.

He saw the man from a long way down the beach. His first impulse was to ignore him. Pretend that he had not seen him. He brought his rod back and cast the dancing rig of bait and weights into the crashing surf. He tried to focus his whole attention on the line between his fingers, the tip of the rod, but his mind kept sliding away, his eyes turning to search for the hunched-over figure. He could not concentrate on the fishing. They had unfinished business. He asked his father to take care of his rod and started off up the beach.

'Didn't know if I'd see you again,' the artist said without looking up.

'You nearly didn't,' Richard replied.

He stood slightly to the side of the artist's chair, looking down at him. The man looked up for a second. His eyes had changed. The glitter had gone from the blackness. They were dull, covered with a haze, like the bloom that grows on autumn sloes. His face was pale beneath the tan, and rigid. Despite the coldness of the wind, sweat sheened his skin. His hair was flecked with paint. The long tangled coils trembled slightly, shaken by a tremor that the man could not control.

'Heard about you finding Clio and Hammond. Bit of a shock for you, was it?'

He laughed, then wiped spittle away from his mouth. If he knew, they all did. But then they had probably known anyway. What a fool he'd been. What a little innocent. Richard could taste the humiliation like metal in his mouth. At least he doesn't know what I had actually thought, Richard reflected; that would really be bad.

'Thought it was me, didn't you?' The artist squinted up at him. 'You've more imagination than I'd have given you credit for. Not possible, old son. I'm impotent, you see. Can't get it up any more.'

Richard didn't know what to say. He stared down at the bone-white cockle shells strewn over the wet sand while his shame returned, threatening to engulf him.

'We all think dark things sometimes. Don't fret yourself about it.'

He coughed and spat a gob of mucus like a miniature jellyfish on to the sand. He's not well, Richard thought. Not well at all. He wondered if he should comment on it. Say something.

'I swim every day I'm here,' the artist had once told him. 'Whatever the weather, whatever the time of year.'

Today was not a good day for swimming. Perhaps he had caught a chill.

The artist turned from the boy to contemplate the sea in front of them.

'I set you up with her. You know that, don't you? With

Clio. I wanted you and her to be together. I wanted her to be with someone her own age. There was an innocence about it that appealed to me. A symmetry. Those games you played. Lovely. That's why I did the drawings. You didn't see it that way. Evidently. Oh, well.' He sighed. 'Call it an experiment that failed.'

Richard did not say anything. He felt used. Abused. By him. By all of them. Any sympathy he'd begun to feel seeped away like water into the sand.

'I've got something to tell you,' the artist said.

Wasn't that enough?

'Something I've never told anybody.'

'Why me?' Richard was unsure if he wanted to hear it.

'Good as anybody.'

There was a tremor in the man's hand as he began to paint. Despite what he was feeling, Richard had to admire his skill. The subtlety he gave to a view which seemed to Richard just dull and grey. He made you see it differently. Richard shifted his stance, deliberately turning his gaze away from the luminosity, the shining pearly quality, growing under the painter's fingers.

'You have no siblings. No brothers or sisters,' the artist went on. 'Didn't you tell me that?'

'Yes,' Richard replied eventually. 'There's only me.'

'In some ways you are lucky. In some ways. I had a brother. You have a look of him. I saw it that first time when you came into the garden.'

Richard said nothing. He knew all this. The man's mind must be wandering. He couldn't decide whether to go or stay.

'He was older than me.' The artist loaded more paint from his palette. 'He drowned. Here. Right off this spot. And I watched. I didn't swim well then and could do noth-

206

ing to save him. That's what I told myself. There was no one around. The beach was deserted. By the time I found help, it was too late. It was not my fault. Amazing the lies you tell yourself. We'd had a quarrel.'

'What about?' Richard asked. The words were out before he could stop himself.

'I have absolutely no idea.' The artist's laugh turned into a wheezing, racking cough. 'Something. Nothing. He hit me, I remember that. Isn't it the way of brothers? What do boys fight about?' He shrugged and wiped his brush on his sleeve to remove excess pigment. 'You look for meaning where there is no meaning. That's what I've come to realize. Perhaps I could have saved him. Although our quarrel was trivial, part of me wanted him to drown.'

'You were too busy saving yourself.'

'You're not so stupid, are you?' The artist looked sideways at Richard, one eyebrow raised, then he went back to his painting. 'I don't know why I'm telling you this.' He stopped, as if gathering his strength. His face was the colour of dirty putty, sweat was rolling down his cheeks in oily droplets. The tremor in his hand was going into spasm, but still he took little specks of colour: blue, red, yellow, and worked them into a sea and sky where Richard could see no colour at all. 'Never told anyone from that day to this. There is no escaping. I want you to know that, Richard.' He looked up at the boy. 'You always have to pay.'

He broke off speaking. His face pulled into a rigid grin as he took in air with a gasping hiss.

'Are you all right?' Richard asked reluctantly, although he obviously wasn't OK.

'Fine as I'll ever be.' The man squinted out to sea. 'The light's changing. The moment's over. One moment. That's all you get. All you can have. One moment good or bad. It's

207

finished now. Finished as it will ever be. Here –' he ripped the page from his book and gave it to the boy – 'you have it. My compliments.'

He looked very bad. His lips had gone a funny colour. Richard did not know the name for the hue: cyan blue? He stared at the painting, not sure why it was being offered, or if he should accept it. In the end he took it and left the man with his hands empty, staring out to sea. When he turned back the chair was vacant. All up and down the beach there was no sign of anyone.

Richard carried on walking, back to his father, back to his fishing. Pages from the artist's notebook were flying in the gusting wind, fluttering and wheeling like gulls on the wing. It could have been raining banknotes. The falling papers were worth a fortune. They landed all around, face down on the sand, on the water, slowly turning to worthless sodden sheets soaked by the rain, washed in and out by the breaking waves.

Richard would go back and continue fishing while his mother packed up the car to go home. When the tide turned and the waves subsided it would be time to reel in the lines and go up to the site. Then his father would hitch the caravan to the towing bar of the Rover and they would be on their way home.

By the next summer, Dylan's plans would be in operation; the plot rents raised so high that Richard's dad would refuse to pay. The caravan would end up resting on bricks on the drive at home. They would never come back here again.

Mermaid

(1976) Oil on canvas

183 x 122 cm

Tate Gallery

J. A. Dalton (1916–1976)

The painting looks the same as when he last saw it. Clio, standing at the window, her chin resting in her cupped hand, her long arms leaning on the sill. She is wearing the shimmery fish gown which is backless, ending below her waist. Her black hair, falling over her shoulders, shines like scales, her dress trails on the floor behind her like a mermaid's tail; but the style of the dress, the curve of her breast, the flare of her hips suggest that Jay has painted her not as a mermaid, or even as the girl she was then, but as the woman that she will become.

The caption reads:

This last painting has been acclaimed by many as Dalton's masterpiece. In it he has combined many of his abiding themes of myth, youth, beauty and loss. The painting has a powerful, haunting quality and the perfectly realized, almost photographic style of the painting give the work a heightened, surreal sensibility that is both aesthetically appealing and profoundly disturbing.

The brass telescope stands to one side, pointing down, sightless and redundant. There is a mirror in front of her, but she gazes past it out to a stormy sea where ships founder and men drown – tiny stick-like arms thrown up in despair, little dark dots of heads, about to disappear under the slate-grey waves. The mirror reflects the room, a dark, domestic space: the world she will leave behind. The artist, a brooding shadowed presence. Leaning closer, Richard can see his portrait in tiny thumbnail miniature.

'He completed it that day,' a voice said behind him. 'That was why he wasn't in the house when you came back.'

Richard continued to look at the work. Clio came up close to him, linking her arm through his. She wore some spicy perfume, less heavy and cloying than the patchouli oil he remembered. He was taller than her now. When he turned round, her hair smelt of meadows and flowers.

She reached up and kissed him on the cheek. Then laughed and rubbed away the purple mark her lips had left there.

'How are you, Richard? What are you doing with yourself?'

'Good. I'm good,' he managed to say.

'I saw you when you first came in. I've been *dying* for a chance to talk. I didn't think you'd come.' She looked at him, her bottom lip caught between her teeth in that way he remembered. 'What are you doing?' She leaned towards him. 'You must tell me all about yourself. I want to know everything.'

She held his arm tighter. He could feel the warmth of her skin through the thin cotton of his shirt as she steered him round the room. They talked of their lives, what they'd been doing since they parted. Clio chatted easily and asked him plenty of questions, but Richard was finding it hard to keep up his end of the conversation. Her nearness was close to rendering him speechless and, although they were surrounded by reminders of that summer, he felt shut down by all the people. There was so much more he wanted to ask her, so much he wanted to say.

Clio talked on, as though they were just casual friends renewing an old acquaintance. He guided her into the area that contained the triptych and held her hands in his. He gazed about at her younger selves looking down on them and asked:

'What's this all about, Clio?'

'I thought . . .' Her eyes skittered from one image to another. 'I thought the act of putting it on walls would also contain it.' She made a sphere with her hands. 'Inside a capsule.'

Richard didn't need to ask more. It was all here in the paintings, the work she had put together. Her pain. His, too.

'Like a therapy?'

'I guess. Although I've had that, too.'

'Has it helped? The show.'

She laughed, but her eyes sparkled with tears. 'A little bit.' She reached out her hand, spanning the space from one side of the triptych to the other. 'These were the paintings you tried to give to Hammond.'

'I was fifteen.' Richard looked away. 'I didn't understand. I didn't know. I had no idea it would affect him that way.' They both knew that he was talking about Jay.

'It didn't. You didn't. You didn't even destroy all the drawings. There were still some in his notebook. You mustn't blame yourself, Richard. None of it was your fault. It was nobody's fault. Not really. You must have heard what happened. Some poisonous species mixed in with the magic mushrooms he collected with Lucia.'

'That's what I read,' Richard said. She was giving the story. The official version. He could tell from her face that there was more to it than that. 'Why weren't you affected?'

'I didn't take them. It was Lucia, Jay and Joe. Joe got up in the middle of the night, complaining of gut ache, saying he didn't feel right. Next thing the ambulance was there. Jay refused to go with them. Said he felt fine.'

'But he wasn't, was he?'

Richard could see Jay's face, grey as ash, his lips turning blue. He could hear the churning waves. Smell the sea.

Do you have things to confess, Richard? Things you feel guilty about? The artist's words came back to him. *I bet you do.*

'I was there with him. Down on the beach,' Richard said. He could barely look at Clio. 'I could see he was in a bad way. I should have done something. Gone for help. Told my dad. Maybe if I had . . .'

'Don't torture yourself. By then he was past help. What he did was clever. He mixed the poisonous species into the mushrooms, just enough to make them all ill, but he took something else, too. He made a decoction from plants in the Witches' Garden. Then he walked into the sea. Just to make sure.'

'But why did he do it?'

'Why does anyone?' She looked up at him. 'He didn't want to live any more.'

Richard shook his head, refusing to accept that it could be as simple as that.

'That's what Lucia says. And she knew him best, so I think we have to accept it. We all blamed ourselves, but really it was nothing to do with us. He lived inside himself. Always had. We were incidental, if that. He lived for his art, nothing else mattered to him. He had the onset of Parkinson's disease, but nobody knew. Meg had her suspicions, but he wouldn't listen. You know what he was like.'

'Why didn't she tell Lucia?'

'He made her promise not to; then it was too late. He'd taken his own steps. It was as if he had a clock ticking away inside him and that day it stopped.'

'But to kill himself! I still don't understand.'

'Neither did I. Then. I was just angry. Angry at everybody. I even blamed you, the way you came into our lives, disturbing the balance somehow. But mostly I was mad at him. How could he do that to me? Lucia helped me to see differently. And Meg. Parkinson's is degenerative and incurable. For an artist to lose the use of his hands . . .'

Richard nodded. What else was there to say?

He looked round. 'Is Meg here? How about Lucia?'

'No.' Clio shook her head. 'Meg's been and gone. She's babysitting tonight. Lucia's in Italy. She's got a new man, and a new baby. Imagine!'

Richard tried, but had difficulty.

'What about Joe?'

'He's in California. He went out there to visit a friend and stayed. He likes the lifestyle. He's got a job now, working for a computer company named after some kind of fruit. Martin's over there . . .'

'Where?'

Richard had been half looking out for him, but hadn't seen him.

'There. Talking to that guy by the wine table.'

Richard looked again. He only recognized him by his thinness. He wore faded jeans ripped at the knees, over high-heeled cowboy boots. His ruffled shirt was open, displaying his bony chest, and he wore his hair shaved up on one side with the other falling long, blond and straight over one mascaraed, kohl-outlined, blue-shadowed eye. He wore a lipstick darker than Clio's and his rouged cheeks showed a dusting of glitter.

'Looks like his skin's cleared,' Richard remarked. 'And he appears to have made up his mind.' He shook his head. 'I can't believe what I said that day.'

'I know.' Clio grinned. 'A lot of your friends are gay.'

'Not *that* many.' He smiled at the cliché. 'But I wouldn't say that kind of thing now, that's for sure.'

He was wondering what he should do, what to say next, when someone came up behind her.

'There you are, my darling. I've been looking for you everywhere. It's time for me to say a few words. Better do it now before they all get too pissed.'

Hammond's baritone purred possession. His blue eyes met Richard's, just for a second, and he smiled as his arms snaked around her slender waist. He bent to nuzzle her neck. She laughed, throaty and deep, like Lucia. She closed her eyes slightly, turning her head to receive his kiss. Richard took advantage of that moment to escape. If she was with him, good luck to her. He obviously really cared for her. What Clio felt was anybody's guess, but he was a handy guy to have as a lover. Making it as any kind of artist was tough.

She caught him outside the door. He had paused there, just long enough to collect himself. It had rained while he was inside and he stood, leaning against the wall, looking at the slippery street, drinking in the cool air.

'It's good to see you again, Richard,' she said, taking his hand and leaning towards him. 'Thanks for coming. I'm really glad you did.'

Then she kissed him. Her lips on his, warm and lingering, bringing back instantly all he remembered of her

215

that summer. He wanted to say something that would keep her with him, but she was already turning away, disappearing back into the crowded gallery. This was her world now, and he wasn't part of it, never could be. Neither would ever forget the other, but their time together was over.

Had she loved him? Probably not. Not in the way he'd loved her. Not in the way he'd wanted, but he no longer blamed her. Love is a profoundly self-regarding emotion; he'd learned that since. He'd learned a lot from Clio, including technique. Plenty of girls had fallen for him, and he'd treated them all badly. Just like she'd done him.

The lights of the gallery spilt across the street. People were leaving, making their goodbyes. For them, this had been just another private view. Jay had wanted to keep the moment, hold on to it forever. In there were some of his attempts to do just that. Richard had argued that it was impossible, but he'd kept going back to that summer. Now he felt he did not have to do that any more. The time had been contained, put in a capsule.

Clever Clio. He really did wish her well.

Her kiss still buzzed on his lips as he set off down the rain-washed, neon-splashed streets. He stood on the corner, deciding which pub to go to, feeling something like release.

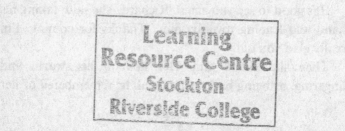

Celia Rees writes for older children and teenagers. Her books have wide popular appeal, combining compelling story-telling with powerful themes and subject matter. For many years she taught English in city comprehensive schools, and she now divides her time between writing and talking to readers in school and libraries. Her acclaimed novels for older children and teenagers include *Witch Child*, *Sorceress*, *Pirates!* and *Truth or Dare*. She lives in Leamington Spa, Warwickshire.

Celia Rees says: 'Everyone has special places, special summers, special people, combined into times they will never forget. Fiction allows the writer to use such times, such places, such people and to blend them together into a story. *The Wish House* is not one place, it is several. The people who live there are fictional, but the events that happen are archetypal: first love, first sex, first death.'

The Wish House is set in the 1970s, when sexual responsibility mainly meant preventing unwanted pregnancy. Today it is also important to prevent sexually transmitted diseases, which means it is essential to use a condom along with any other method of birth control.

A selected list of titles available from Macmillan Children's Books

The prices shown below are correct at the time of going to press. However, Macmillan Publishers reserves the right to show new retail prices on covers which may differ from those previously advertised.

Celia Rees

| Truth or Dare | 0 330 36875 3 | £4.99 |
| The Bailey Game | 0 330 39830 X | £4.99 |

Julie Bertagna

The Opposite of Chocolate	0 330 39746 X	£4.99
Exodus	0 330 39908 X	£5.99
Sugar Rush	0 330 41583 2	£4.99

All Pan Macmillan titles can be ordered from our website,
www.panmacmillan.com, or from your local bookshop
and are also available by post from:

Bookpost, PO Box 29, Douglas, Isle of Man IM99 1BQ
Credit cards accepted. For details:
Telephone: 01624 677237
Fax: 01624 670923
Email: bookshop@enterprise.net
www.bookpost.co.uk

Free postage and packing in the United Kingdom